The Intruder

Cedar River Daydreams

Other Books by Judy Baer

The Intruder

Judy Baer

BETHANY HOUSE PUBLISHERS
MINNEAPOLIS, MINNESOTA 55438

The Intruder
Judy Baer

Library of Congress Catalog Card Number 89–61623

ISBN 1-55661-088-2

Published by Bethany House Publishers
A Division of Bethany Fellowship, Inc.
6820 Auto Club Road, Minneapolis, Minnesota 55438

Printed in the United States of America

For friends far away but close to my heart—
Mary Dodd and Mary Matteson

JUDY BAER received a B.A. in English and Education from Concordia College in Moorhead, Minnesota. She has had fifteen novels published and is a member of the National Romance Writers of America, the Society of Children's Book Writers and the National Federation of Press Women.

Two of her novels have been prizewinning best-sellers in the Bethany House SPRINGFLOWER SERIES (for girls 12–15); *Adrienne* and *Paige*. Both books have been awarded first place for juvenile fiction in the National Federation of Press Women's communications contest.

Chapter One

"Gotta go, Mom! Todd just drove up." Lexi glanced out the front window and waved at Todd Winston as he drove his navy blue '49 Ford coupe to the curb in front of the Leighton's house.

Lexi pulled a brush through her thick brown hair and darted to the hall closet for a jacket.

"What did you say, Lexi?" Mrs. Leighton meandered into the foyer, her hair touseled and sprouting in a dozen directions, her hands full of paint brushes loaded with cobalt, umber and sienna.

"I'm leaving. Todd's here." Lexi smoothed the front of her teal colored jumper and examined herself in the mirror. She'd made the jumper herself and was rather pleased with the results.

"Why?"

Lexi bit back an impatient remark. Her mother had been so absent-minded these past few days!

"There's an Emerald Tones rehearsal tonight at seven at the school. Remember? I told you about it at breakfast this morning. Todd is here to pick me up. He's waiting outside right now."

"Oh yes." Mrs. Leighton gave a small shrug. "You said something about a concert coming up soon."

"If we can get ready. Mrs. Waverly is very fussy about our sound. She calls us the 'cream of the crop.' " Lexi grinned. "I guess that's why she doesn't want us to go sour."

Mrs. Leighton smiled vaguely and Lexi suspected her mother hadn't comprehended the joke, even if it *was* a sick one. In fact, Lexi mused, her mother didn't seem to hear or enjoy much of anything lately. All she did was paint listlessly on the stacks of stretched and gessoed canvases she'd accumulated in the small den off the living room. The entire Leighton family was breathing paint thinner day and night.

"Where's your father?" Mrs. Leighton asked Lexi. "I haven't seen him since supper."

"He and Ben are out back building a bird house. I heard him yelling once. I think Dad hit his hand with a hammer."

"I hope Ben doesn't get hurt," Mrs. Leighton fretted. "He's not very old to be working with those kinds of tools."

"He's eight, going on nine," Lexi reminded her mother. "And very coordinated, considering." It usually fell to Lexi to remind her mother not to overprotect Ben. Even though he was a Down's syndrome child, Ben was very quick and especially handy with tools of any sort.

Mrs. Leighton looked wistfully at Lexi and then at Todd waiting in the street. "Will you be late? It seems like a long time since you and I had a heart-to-heart talk."

Lexi leaned forward and gave her mother a kiss

on the cheek. "I'll hurry. I promise. Don't go to bed until I get back."

"It's a deal. Have fun, honey."

Lexi's head bobbed in agreement. She left the house and turned back to wave with a cheerfulness she didn't feel. She wished that she had time to talk to mother now, that she could draw out of Mrs. Leighton what it was that was bothering her these past few days, but . . . Lexi looked anxiously to the street. Todd was waiting.

"Hiya, Lex," Todd greeted her. "Ready to sing your heart out?" His dark blue eyes smiled at her. "You look great tonight. New outfit?"

"I made it this afternoon."

"You're kidding, right?" Todd looked impressed.

"No. I cut it out last night, so all I had to do was sew it together. It was easy. No zippers or sleeves."

"You're something else, Lexi," Todd said with admiration. "I tried to sew on a button once."

"What happened?"

"I poked my finger and bled on the shirt. I ended up wearing one of Dad's."

Lexi giggled. "Thanks. I needed that."

"Needed what?" Todd looked puzzled and gave her a sideways glance as he eased the car out into the road.

"I needed to laugh. There's not much laughter at our house these days."

"Trouble? Somebody sick?"

"No. Not really. Just . . . weirdness."

"Who's turning weird? Not Ben!"

Lexi smiled. "Never Ben. He's always exactly the same. If everyone had a disposition as sweet as Ben's, we'd have peace in the world today. Actually, it's my mom."

"Your mom?" Todd echoed. "I can't believe that! She's a great lady."

"I know, but lately she's been acting bored or depressed or *something*." Lexi crossed her arms and burrowed deeper into the velvety cushion of the old car's seat. "Actually, I think she's looking for something important to do."

"Important? She's a terrific artist—even my parents say so. And she's a great mother—you say that."

"I know. She's the best. When we first moved to Cedar River and I was having problems finding friends, I was really glad my mom was there for me. And she loves to do things with Ben. She's even teaching him to paint. So far, though, he's gotten more on himself than on the canvas. We have an entire collection of purple cows with green horns, compliments of Ben."

"So what's the problem?"

Lexi chewed thoughtfully on her lower lip. "I think the problem is that there's *no* problem."

"Huh?"

"Ben's happy at the Academy. He's doing much better than either Mom or Dad anticipated he would. I'm assistant photographer for the school newspaper and was selected for the Emerald Tones. Between you and the rest of my friends, I'm hardly home after school. As far as I can tell, Mom thinks she doesn't have enough to do!"

Todd pulled into the high school parking lot and flicked off the ignition. He laid his arm across the back of the seat and turned to face Lexi. "So, what can you do about that?"

Lexi shrugged. "Wait for it to pass, I guess. I had lots of trouble when I first moved here. Remember how rotten Minda Hannaford was to me? But, in time, it has all worked out. I guess that's what will have to happen for Mom."

Todd ran the tip of his index finger across Lexi's cheek. "Let me know if there's anything I can do to help, okay?"

Lexi shot him an appreciative glance. "Thanks."

Before he could respond, Jennifer Golden poked her blond head through the window of the driver's seat. "Hey, you two! What are you talking about?" She blew a big pink bubble of gum. When it snapped, it caught on her nose.

"Who says it's any of your business, Golden?" Todd retorted cheerfully as he opened the door and slid out.

"Anything to do with you two is my business," Jennifer shot back as she pulled the bubble gum off her nose. "That's what best friends are for."

"Then, if you're such a good friend, why aren't you at home finishing my history assignment?" Todd asked.

Jennifer snorted. "You want *me* to do *your* work? Aren't you afraid it might come out all backward?" She screwed up her face and flapped her hands in the air and tilted her head to one side. "Like me?"

"You can't get my sympathy that way," Todd retorted. "You're dyslexic, not dumb."

"Oh, well then. . . ." Jennifer flashed a grin between Todd and Lexi. "Lighten up, you two! We're going to discuss our *tour*!"

The threesome made their way into the school

and down the long halls to the music room. They entered just as Mrs. Waverly was clearing her throat to plead for silence.

"I'd like your attention, please!" Mrs. Waverly's beige hair was piled high on her head, and tilting slightly, like the Leaning Tower of Pisa. She had two pencils and a red marking pen stuck through the curls. Lexi covered her mouth to hide a smile.

Mrs. Waverly was one of the most popular teachers in school. No one even seemed to mind that by the end of a hard day, Mrs. Waverly might have enough pens and pencils stuck through her hair to supply an entire class.

"Where are we going on tour?" someone at the back of the room asked.

"Bernersville, Plattstown and Porter. We'll be staying overnight in Plattstown after the evening concert there and going on to Porter for a lyceum in the school gymnasium before returning to Cedar River. . . ."

"Awright! We'll be missing two days of school!"

Mrs. Waverly dug into her file for a memorandum. "About that . . . the principal has said we can go *only* if everyone completes their assignments two days prior to departure. . . ."

While most of the students groaned, Lexi and Todd only smiled and looked at each other. Homework or not, this sounded like it was going to be fun.

"When do we leave?" Todd asked.

"The date hasn't been set yet," Mrs. Waverly explained. "We want to coordinate things in all three towns at once, so it's taking a bit of extra work. I'll let you know as soon as everything is finalized."

The next half hour was filled with excited questions about the tour and the arrangements Mrs. Waverly had made. Then, when the discussion was completed, they rehearsed the program that they'd sing. It was after nine-thirty when Todd and Lexi returned to the Leighton household.

"Looks dark," Todd observed.

"Ben's in bed, that's all. I'm sure Mom is up. Come in and have something to eat."

"Are you sure?"

"Of course." Lexi led the way to the kitchen where Mrs. Leighton was just taking a pan of fragrant chocolate chip cookies from the oven.

"Is that what I think it is?" Todd said hungrily.

"Help yourself." Mrs. Leighton waved her spatula toward the cookies. "How was the rehearsal?"

"Great!" Lexi plopped herself down on a stool and took a cookie in each hand. "We're going to be gone two days. Everybody has to get their work done in advance and—"

"Two days?" Mrs. Leighton frowned. "Where will you stay?"

"Homes. Mrs. Waverly has it all worked out. Jennifer and I will be rooming together. Isn't that great? We've already figured out that I'll bring my blow dryer and she'll bring her travel iron so we won't have to carry so much stuff."

"You sharing toothbrushes, too?" Todd asked playfully.

Lexi tossed a cookie at him which he caught deftly. "What do you think?"

They were talking so animatedly about the tour that it was some moments before either of them realized that Mrs. Leighton had hardly said a word.

Todd, glancing from Lexi to her mother and back again, finally murmured, "I think I'd better be going." He slid off the stool. "Thanks for the cookies, Mrs. Leighton, they were great."

"Uhmmm . . . you're welcome." Mrs. Leighton's eyes barely focused on Todd as she spoke to him. Her mind could have been a million miles away.

Lexi followed Todd as he made his way to the front door.

"See what I mean?" she whispered.

Todd nodded and his expression was grim. "She really is acting different. She's usually not so *quiet*."

"Maybe we were just especially noisy tonight?" Lexi wondered hopefully.

"Maybe."

But Lexi knew that wasn't true. Her mother definitely had something troubling on her mind.

When Todd was gone, Lexi returned to the kitchen where her mother was cleaning up the cooking utensils.

"Mom, what do you think about this tour?" Lexi curled herself around a stool and leaned her elbows on the counter.

"I'm sure it will be great fun for you, dear." Mrs. Leighton paused to stare out the window into the darkness. "But it will be lonesome here without you."

"It's only for two days!"

"True. And you're hardly here as it is. . . ." Mrs. Leighton managed a weak smile. "I'm very glad you're having this opportunity."

Very glad? Lexi wondered as she mounted the stairs to her bedroom. Her mother looked anything *but* very glad to have her daughter taking a trip—even one only two days long.

Lexi threw herself onto the bed, cupped her hands beneath her head and stared at the ceiling.

"Oh, Lord," she finally prayed. "Help my mom. Bring into her life whatever it is she needs to feel useful again. She's the greatest mother in the world, Lord. Thanks for giving her to Ben and me. Help her to know how much we love her."

Feeling better, Lexi rolled off the bed and reached for her pajamas. God would take care of her mom. There was no doubt about that.

Chapter Two

The next morning Lexi didn't have time to think about her mother or her problems. It was nearly 7:30 A.M. when Lexi realized that she had turned off her alarm clock at its first ring and fallen back to sleep. She raced through her shower and dressed in record time. Her family was just sitting up to the breakfast table when she arrived in the kitchen.

"Juice, Lexi?" her mother asked. "How about pancakes?"

"No, thanks, not today. My stomach is still racing to catch up with the rest of me. Why didn't someone wake me up?"

Mrs. Leighton looked up in surprise, "I heard your alarm go off. I didn't realize that you'd over-slept."

"That's okay," Lexi said. "But I still think I'll just have juice."

"Breakfast is good for you, Lexi," Ben pointed out in a childish warble.

She looked at the shining cap of his dark head and the expectant expression on his face. "Oh, all right Ben. I guess I'll have a pancake. Just one."

Ben nodded approvingly and returned to his own meal as Lexi sank into the chair next to him. She still felt rushed when her father dropped her off at the school and Binky McNaughton met her in the doorway.

"Hi, Lexi. What's wrong with you?" Binky inquired cheerfully. "You look like you've been running a race."

"I feel like I have," Lexi groaned. "I overslept this morning."

Binky gave an unladylike snort. "Sounds good to me. You can't sleep in our house. Egg thinks it's his job to wake up the birds in our yard. I heard his alarm go off at five this morning."

Egg McNaughton, Binky's brother, was a tall, lanky beanpole of a boy with an excess of nervous energy.

"You know, sometimes I think he just does things to irritate me. He knows I don't want to get up at five o'clock in the morning, but he always pounds on my door like it's his duty to get me out of bed."

Lexi smiled. Binky, a tiny bird-like girl, and her brother Egg were very fond of each other. They were also fond of the constant brother/sister sparring that went on between them. Binky and Egg were perfectly willing to criticize each other. However, if a third party were to say something negative about either of them, they would leap to their family member's defense.

"That Egg just drives me crazy sometimes," Binky complained. "He's always doing something weird. Do you know what he's eating for breakfast these days?"

Lexi mutely shook her head. She was sure she was going to find out.

"He calls it a health drink. I don't know whose health it's supposed to help. It's the most gross thing you've ever seen. He mixes up yogurt and wheat germ and vitamin C crystals and juice and a raw egg and—"

Lexi held up her hand. "Stop! I don't want to hear anymore."

Binky nodded sagely. "I know, but Egg drinks it every morning. You know what? I think he thinks it's gonna give him . . ." she paused and whispered conspiratorily, "muscles."

Lexi almost laughed out loud. The idea of a muscular Egg seemed incongruous. Egg was built like the stick figures that she used to draw on the back of her notebooks in grade school. Tall, pencil thin and gangly.

"He's been lifting weights, too," Binky confided. "I'm not supposed to tell. He ordered a set of weights through the catalog and he has them set up in the basement. He goes down there and I hear horrible sounds coming up the stairs—groans and grunts. . . ."

"Are you sure you should be telling me this?" Lexi wondered. She was not particularly anxious to hear about Egg's health regime, particularly if it was supposed to be a secret.

Binky shrugged. "I have to tell somebody. It's just so strange. He's drinking that awful concoction and lifting weights and asking my mom if she couldn't please serve some sprouts on the salad at supper."

"Maybe Egg's getting into physical fitness," Lexi pointed out matter-of-factly.

"Maybe," Binky agreed. "But there's another reason other than good health if Egg is going to all this trouble. I think it must be a girl, don't you?"

Lexi smiled. "Minda Hannaford, you mean?"

Binky nodded forlornly. "I don't suppose he'll ever get over that crush he has on Minda. And most likely what's going to happen is that he's either going to hurt himself or make himself sick doing these things before Minda has a chance to notice that he ever developed any muscles."

"Well, I think it's great," Lexi defended. "At least he's doing something to improve himself. We could all use a little of that."

"Yeah," Binky said gloomily. "Especially Minda. She should start an exercise program for her personality to see if she could improve it."

"Now, Bink," Lexi began, but she really couldn't say more. Minda wasn't the sweetest person in the world and Lexi had a feeling she would never try to change.

A little sigh escaped Lexi. Binky turned toward her friend and said, "Something the matter?"

"Oh no, not really," Lexi said. "I was just thinking about Peggy."

"Yeah. I wonder how she likes living with her uncle," Binky said enthusiastically. Then she frowned. "I sure miss having her around here, though."

Lexi nodded silently. She missed her friend Peggy, too. Very few people besides Lexi, Todd and Chad Allen, Peggy's boyfriend, knew that Peggy had left Cedar River to go and live with her uncle in Arizona and give birth to a baby. Everyone else believed she'd gone to live with her uncle while her parents went to London to do research on a book her father was writing.

Peggy was one of the first girls that had befriended Lexi when she came to Cedar River. It left a real empty spot in her life not to have Peggy around to talk to.

"She'll be back in the fall, won't she?" Binky asked curiously.

Lexi nodded.

"I'm glad." Binky slammed her locker door shut and hoisted a mound of books higher in her skinny arms.

"Are you going to class?" Lexi eyed Binky's armful of books. "What about that make-up Phy. Ed. class? Don't we have that first thing this morning?"

Binky groaned. "I forgot all about that. Yuk, I hate Phy. Ed. I suppose he'll make us do something horrible, like run relays."

"Actually, I think we're supposed to be playing basketball."

Binky rolled her eyes. "Worse yet. All I do is trip on my own two feet."

———

Binky was as good as her word. She'd stumbled half a dozen times in her few minutes on the court as a guard while Lexi watched from the side lines, awaiting her turn.

Lexi and Minda Hannaford had been placed on the same team. Lexi didn't know if that was good or bad. It was almost as hard to play *with* Minda as against her.

Minda scooted across the bench toward Lexi. "So, Lexi, did you get any good photos for the next school paper?"

Lexi nodded. "Todd did. I haven't taken many this week, but I plan to take a lot of them when the Emerald Tones go on tour. That should be good for an entire series, don't you think?"

Minda shrugged. She wasn't particularly interested in the Emerald Tones since she was not a member. It was Minda's style to place importance and priority only on the things that she herself was involved in.

"Come on girls, you're in," the Phy. Ed. teacher said with a wave toward Lexi and Minda. Without much enthusiasm, Lexi jumped up and headed for the center of the court. Minda, who had appointed herself team captain, was already shouting out instructions concerning who should handle the ball and where it should be shot from.

Almost immediately, the ball was passed to Lexi and she brought it down court toward their team's basket. She could hear Minda shouting in the background. "Don't shoot, Lexi, don't shoot! You'll never make it! Pass it off! Shoot it to me! I'll put in! I'll put in!"

Though Lexi was sure she could have made the basket, she passed it off to Minda who managed to dribble weakly under the basket, toss it up and have it bounce off the backboard and onto the stage.

"You should have passed it sooner, Lexi," Minda chastised.

"Or not at all," Lexi muttered under her breath.

It was barely nine-thirty in the morning and already Minda was getting on Lexi's nerves. With each passing week of school, Lexi lost more and more hope that she and Minda would ever become friends. There had been a time in Minda's life when her parents were separating and she'd had nowhere to turn so she had confided in Lexi, but ever since that day it seemed the two girl's relationship had grown more and more distant.

Lexi gave a thankful sigh of relief when the bell rang and the girls were all dismissed to go into the locker room and change for class.

"It was even worse than I thought, wasn't it?" Binky said sourly. "Phy. Ed. is so . . . yuk!"

"Maybe you should start lifting some of Egg's weights," Lexi chided gently. "Then you might not hate it so much."

"Well, didn't you hate it today?" Binky asked pointedly.

"I did, but not because I don't enjoy basketball."

Binky nodded sagely, "Because of Minda."

Lexi rolled her eyes. "How could you tell?"

"I saw you two in deep conversation more than once. Every time you tried to set up a play, Minda would set up one of her own."

"Do you think that has anything to do with the fact that your team beat us thirty-five to zero?" Lexi asked with a hint of sarcasm in her voice.

"Too many leaders and not enough followers," Binky diagnosed. "You should know better by now than to try and tell Minda how to do anything."

"But she can't even play basketball!" Lexi protested.

Binky shrugged. "So? That doesn't stop her from being bossy!"

Lexi was still upset when she arrived in Mrs. Drummond's English class, nearly two hours later.

"Today we're going to work on play writing," Mrs. Drummond began. "I'd like to take the discussion we had yesterday about play writing and the three-act structure and have you work in sections creating your own plays. Number off from one to five and then divide into groups. Group number one will be here at the front of the room; group number two in the back; group number three under the window; group number four at my desk; and group number five in the center of the room. Now, if you'll all start numbering. . . ."

The class did as Mrs. Drummond said. Much to Lexi's dismay, both she and Minda were in group number three.

Today is just not my day, Lexi decided. First, oversleeping. Now, a double dose of Minda. By the time Lexi had pulled a chair up to the rest of the group, Minda had already taken charge and was saying, "I think we should do a comedy. Something funny. After all, school is such a drag and we need to lighten things up."

"I think drama is a little easier to write, Minda," Lexi pointed out softly.

Minda glanced at Lexi briefly and gave a sharp shake of her head. "Comedy. That's what we want to write, isn't it?" Minda's eyes scanned the small cluster of students.

It was no use, Lexi thought to herself. Minda always managed to get her way by coaxing or sometimes by pure intimidation. They'd be writing a comedy because Minda wanted to no matter what any of the rest of them thought.

Fortunately, Lexi's day ended far better than it had started because she had Emerald Tone rehearsal immediately after school. She was feeling more like her normally cheerful self by the time she reached home. Supper was already on the table and Ben was banging the tip of his fork against the tabletop saying in a sing-song voice, "Ben's hungry, Ben's hungry, Ben's hungry."

"You'd better sit up," Mr. Leighton warned, "otherwise Ben is going to start eating the tablecloth."

"Sorry, I didn't realize I was so late."

"You're not late. I'm just a little early with dinner tonight," Mrs. Leighton said as she brought a large platter of pot roast and potatoes to the table. "Let's say grace, so we can eat before the food gets cold."

"Let's sing," Ben rejoined and held out his hands.

Lexi liked it when her family sang the table blessing. She liked to hear her dad's low rumbling voice and her mother's high, sweet one blending in song.

Ben was always unaffectedly off-key and Lexi's own clear soprano joined in. As soon as Ben had a few bites of food, he laid down his fork, folded his arms across his chest and said, "Guess what?"

Three pair of eyes turned toward Ben. "What, Ben?"

"No, you guess," Ben insisted. "Guess what?"

Lexi sighed. She knew Ben would persist in his game until she started making guesses about what had happened to him in school that day. "You played hooky and you didn't go to the Academy at all," she said.

Ben giggled and shook his head.

"You had buffalo burgers for lunch and you thought they were good," she guessed again.

Ben wrinkled his nose and shook his head emphatically.

"A rocket ship landed on the playground and you had a spaceman come inside for show and tell."

Ben's dark eyes sparkled with glee. "Wrong, Lexi. Lexi's all wrong!"

"All right, then, Ben. You tell me what happened."

Ben clapped his hands together. "Ben was teacher's helper today."

"You were? Good for you, Ben," Lexi said.

"That's my boy," Mr. Leighton chimed.

"What does teacher's helper do, Ben?" Mrs. Leighton wondered.

"Clean erasers," Ben said. "Put away the clay and turn the lights out."

"You did all that, Ben?" Lexi asked.

Ben nodded proudly.

"Well, it sounds like Ben had a wonderful day," Mr. Leighton concluded. "How about you, Lexi? How was your day?"

Lexi wrinkled her nose. She didn't want to get into the hassles she had had with Minda. Instead, she brought up the Emerald Tone rehearsal. "We practiced for the tour again after school. Things are sounding better every time we go through them. I think it's going to be great." A frown flitted across Lexi's face. "I'm a little worried though."

"What about?"

"Well, we're supposed to bring our own spending money. Mrs. Waverly said that our meals would be provided, but if we want to do any shopping—"

"You're going to get time to shop?" Mrs. Leighton wondered. "I thought this was a working tour."

"Still, I hope I have enough money to take along. I just spent a lot of it on fabric to sew school clothes. Money just doesn't seem to go as far as it used to," Lexi observed.

Mr. Leighton burst out laughing. "You've noticed that too, Lexi? When the economy crunch filters all the way down to the nation's teenagers, we know it's getting serious."

"Maybe I should quit going to the Hamburger Shack after school," Lexi mused. "But everyone does it and we really have a good time and—"

"I doubt that's necessary, Lexi," Mr. Leighton assured her.

"I don't know, Dad. It seems like by the time I get to Thursday or Friday, my allowance is gone and I still have a day or two to wait before I can collect again."

Mr. Leighton smiled. "Well, maybe you've forgotten, but I still have that job for you at my veterinary office whenever you want to take it."

Lexi's eyes grew round. "You mean it, Dad? I thought you'd probably found someone else by now."

Mr. Leighton shook his head. "We still need a 'gopher,' Lexi. Someone to go for this and go for that. My helpers have too much to do most of the time to run errands. So, if you'd like to earn a little money—"

"Would I ever! Exactly what would I have to do?"

"Errands mostly. Delivering medication occasionally, going to the post office or the drug store, answering the telephone when my secretary's on her break, and it would be nice to have one person in charge of feeding the animals in the evening before we close."

"That'd be great, Dad. I'd love to do that. It wouldn't seem like work at all. Just think, I could earn money while having fun!"

Lexi's father laughed. "Well, I doubt it would be that much fun, but I would like to see you earning some of your spending money." He smiled. "I believe that I could even pay you well enough so that you could put some away for college, too."

Ben, who had been listening quietly to this exchange, finally piped up. "Me, too."

"You too, what, Ben?" his father asked.

"Me, too. Ben wants a job. I can feed animals."

"Uh, well, yes, I'm sure you could, Ben. But don't you think you're a little young to have a job?"

Ben solemnly shook his head, his dark hair glinting in the light. "Ben's not too young. Ben needs a job, too."

"Looking for a little extra spending money, are you son?" Mr. Leighton asked.

Ben's eyes grew wide. "What's spending money?"

Mr. Leighton chuckled. "It's the money you put in your piggy bank. When you take it out and buy candy with it or a toy, then it's called spending money."

Ben thought about that for a long moment. Then he smiled, "Ben doesn't spend his money."

Mr. Leighton looked across the table at his wife.

"I think Ben's got the best idea of all."

Ben clapped his hands together to recapture his father's attention. "Ben wants a job too."

Mr. Leighton looked thoughtful. "Well, let me see. What kind of a job would Ben be good at?"

"Feed the animals," Ben chimed.

"No, I think I'll have Lexi do that. But I know something your mother would like some help with."

"What's that, Dad?" Lexi wondered.

"Well, I think that she'd like to have someone help her take out the garbage. What do you think about that, dear?"

Mrs. Leighton was smiling at the exchange. "I think that would be wonderful. Do you think you could take out the garbage, Ben?"

Ben bobbed his head enthusiastically and pushed himself away from the table.

"Where are you going, Benjamin?" his mother asked.

Ben stared at her with large, brown eyes. "Take out garbage."

"Tell you what, Ben. You help me clean up after supper and then I'll have a garbage bag ready for you to take out. How does that sound?"

"Okay."

"Hey, Ben," Lexi prodded. "Aren't you going to ask him how much you're going to get paid for your job? You'd better ask for at least a nickel a bag."

Ben turned expectantly toward his father and Mr. Leighton threw his hands in the air. "I give up. You two are going to be economists or bankers and I'm just a simple veterinarian. A nickel a bag it is, Ben. Starting right after supper tonight."

"All right," Ben whooped. "Let's make lots of garbage."

The entire Leighton family was laughing over Ben's suggestion when the door bell rang. Lexi jumped up and went to answer it.

Jennifer Golden was standing on the other side of the door tapping her toe impatiently. "Hi," she said as she stepped inside. "I thought I'd better come over so we could talk about what we're taking for the tour." She whipped a small notebook and a pen out of the pocket of her jacket. "I mean, really, Mrs. Waverly said all we get to take is one small carry-on. We're gonna have to plan carefully if that's all we can bring along."

"We've just finished supper," Lexi informed her friend. "I have to do the dishes."

Jennifer shrugged. "That's okay. I'll help you. We had take-out chicken at our house tonight, so I got out of doing them at home." She followed Lexi into the kitchen and grabbed a dish towel from the towel rack next to the sink. "You wash, I'll dry."

Lexi filled the sink with soap bubbles and warm water and began to wash the dishes that Mrs. Leighton carried in from the dining room. Ben danced and pranced underfoot singing "I'm the garbage man" in an off-key tune. It was nearly seven-thirty by the time the girls finished the dishes and Ben had made a huge production of carrying two plastic sacks full of garbage to the cans in the alley.

"Come on," Lexi whispered to Jennifer. "Let's go upstairs before Ben has us crumpling up newspapers to make another bag of garbage."

Jennifer smiled and shook her head. "Lexi, that

little brother of yours is really something, isn't he?"

Lexi nodded and smiled, remembering the first time Jennifer and Ben had met and how uncomfortable Jennifer had been about the fact that Ben was retarded. Now Ben had worked his way into Jennifer's heart.

Upstairs, Jennifer threw open the door to Lexi's closet and stared inside. "You have so many neat clothes, Lexi Leighton. I can't believe it."

"You could too, Jennifer. I could teach you how to sew."

Jennifer held up a hand. "No thanks. I think I'd rather have a sparse wardrobe. What you do looks too hard."

"Well, you don't have to start out with complicated patterns," Lexi pointed out.

"Maybe someday," Jennifer rejoined, "but right now, we've gotta figure out what we're gonna take on the tour. If I were you, I'd take this and this and . . ." She began pulling outfits out of the closet and tossing them onto the bed.

"All that won't fit into one carry-on," Lexi pointed out. "Besides, we have our Emerald Tone jackets. All we really need is a dark skirt and a white blouse to go under the blazer."

"Practical as usual," Jennifer groaned. "Well, get out your suitcase and let's see how much we can cram into it."

The two girls worked on plotting and planning their wardrobe for nearly an hour before Jennifer announced that she had to go home.

Lexi walked her friend downstairs and to the front door. She waved goodbye as Jennifer disappeared down the sidewalk. Still smiling, Lexi closed the front door and glanced toward the living room. "Mom? Are you in there?" Lexi peered into the darkness. "Why are all the lights off?" Lexi fumbled for a table lamp near the doorway.

"Just thinking, that's all. I didn't need lights to do that," her mother explained.

Still, it gave Lexi an eerie feeling to think of her mother sitting alone in the dark. What *was* it that she was thinking about?

Chapter Three

The alarm rang at five A.M. Lexi groaned and rolled over in her bed, pulling her feather pillow close around her ears.

"Go away," she muttered. "Too early."

But the alarm persisted. Soon Mrs. Leighton was knocking at Lexi's door. "Come on, honey. Time to get up. Today's the big tour."

"I don't want to go." Lexi's mumbled into her pillow.

"Sure you do. You'll feel better after you've had a shower." Lexi peered at the face of the clock with a baleful look. It was going to take more than a shower to make her feel better about getting up.

Two glasses of orange juice and a bran muffin later, Lexi was still yawning. Her overnight carry-on was resting next to the back door. Mrs. Leighton was hunting for her car keys.

"If I don't find them soon, you're going to be late," she murmured. "Where did I put them?"

"If I'm late, I'm going back to bed," Lexi concluded. "Don't look too hard."

"Why are you so sleepy this morning?"

Lexi groaned and ran her fingers through her hair. "I couldn't get to sleep last night. I kept thinking about the concert and how much fun it was going to be—"

"And now you want to stay home and go back to sleep?"

Lexi smiled. Even as weary as she was, she had to agree—it didn't make sense to stay home now.

"Maybe I can sleep on the bus?"

"I wouldn't count on it."

Lexi poured a half-inch of juice into her glass and drank it. "Unrealistic, I know. Let's go."

The foyer of the gymnasium was already filling with sleepy students and their parents. Jennifer Golden was just waving goodbye to her parents. Todd had driven himself, Lexi deduced when she saw his '49 Ford parked in the student parking lot.

"Bye, Mom. And thanks." Lexi gave her mother a quick peck on the cheek.

"Have fun."

Lexi nodded. Then she reached out and grasped her mother's forearm. "You have fun *too,* Mom. It seems like you haven't been having much lately."

Mrs. Leighton gave her daughter an impulsive hug. "You're so special, Lexi. I thank God every day for you."

Lexi watched her mother wind her way through the mounds of pillows, blankets and overnight bags to the front door before she turned to look for Jennifer.

"Well, this is it!" Jennifer crowed. "Tour time!"

She unplugged the earphones from her head and did a scuffling little dance.

"You wake up cheerful," Todd observed as he strolled up to the two girls. He was wearing a blue sweatshirt that did incredible things for his eyes.

"You forgot to comb your hair," Jennifer pointed out bluntly.

"So did you."

"Hey! I worked hours to get mine to look like this!"

"So did I."

Lexi held up her hands between the two of them. "Break it up, kiddies. Mrs. Waverly is trying to speak."

Mrs. Waverly had climbed atop a pile of suitcases containing music and was waving her arms in the air. It was the first time Lexi had seen her teacher in anything but dress clothes. Mrs. Waverly was wearing a pink jogging suit and she had a stretchy pink headband woven through the curls in her hair.

"How old is Mrs. Waverly?" Lexi wondered to Jennifer.

She shrugged. "I don't know. Thirty. Forty. Fifty."

"That's no help!"

"I can never tell with teachers, you know? They all seem really *old* when they're in class, but sometimes, when you see them at the mall or a movie they actually look *young*." Jennifer squinted at Mrs. Waverly. "She really looks pretty good, don't you think?"

Obviously Jennifer wasn't going to be any help, Lexi decided. Maybe Mrs. Waverly wasn't thirty anymore, but she wasn't fifty either. And she did look rather pretty in her pink jogging suit.

"Take your bags to the bus driver. He will load them for us. Then, in an orderly fashion, please get on the bus. We will have to be boarded in fifteen minutes in order to stay on schedule."

Lexi and Jennifer found seats together near the back of the bus. Todd and Harry Cramer, a senior with a beautiful tenor voice, sat across from them.

Immediately, Jennifer began to make herself at home. She pulled a bag of corn chips out of her duffle bag, fluffed her pillow and stuffed her lap blanket into the curve of her back. Then, after kicking off her tennis shoes, she stuck her stockinged feet over the seat and into the face of the people in front of her.

"Awright, Golden! Quit it!"

"Quit what?" Jennifer asked innocently.

"Your feet stink!"

"They're clean socks. Washed only last month."

Lexi rolled her eyes and sank deeply into her seat. It was going to be a very long two days.

They were just fifteen miles out of Bernersville when Mrs. Waverly stood up and clapped for attention.

"We'll be at our destination in about twenty minutes. Please start picking up the pop cans and bags of chips that seem to have multiplied since we got on the bus. We'll have lunch at the school and dress there for our first performance. Now if anyone. . . ."

Mrs. Waverly's voice was drowned out by the excited buzz in the bus. With a smile, she sank into her seat, shaking her head.

"Well, Harry, are you ready for this?" Jennifer leaned across Lexi to inquire of the boy sitting next to Todd.

"Sure. Should be easy."

"But you've got a solo."

Harry grinned and the chip he'd gotten in his front tooth playing football showed. "I'm not a shy, shrinking violet like you, Golden."

Todd and Lexi both laughed at that. Lexi liked Harry. He was good-natured and even-tempered and she knew that Todd hung out with him sometimes. Any friend of Todd's was a friend of hers.

Lexi's gaze traveled over the students on the bus. There were so many she still didn't know very well, but gradually she was becoming a part of Cedar River. She rarely thought of Grover's Point anymore. She still wrote letters to all her friends there, but sometimes they seemed so distant—almost unreal. Reality was here now.

———

"Ready?" Todd asked. He was adjusting his tie beneath the trim-fitting green Emerald Tone jacket.

"I think I'm going to throw up."

"Nervous?"

"You bet," Lexi groaned. "And that salmon loaf and green peas they fed us for lunch didn't exactly make my stomach feel great either."

"There should be a law against salmon loaf," Jennifer agreed. "And green beans and lime jello. Humans shouldn't ingest that stuff."

"What'dya mean?" Harry interrupted. "I *like* all that stuff."

Jennifer eyed his massive frame. "You're so big it all probably falls into your right leg and never even hits your stomach. Trust me, salmon loaf is deadly."

The conversation wasn't making Lexi feel any better. What *did* help was the gentle squeeze Todd gave her just before they marched on stage to begin their concert. It also helped that their first group was all grade school and high school students. Lexi could see many impressed expressions on the faces in the audience.

———

Back in the bus, Mrs. Waverly climbed onto a front seat and clapped her hands. "Excellent job, people! Excellent! If you do this well again tonight, I think we can count on being asked back next year!" She eyed the group. "And because I heard most of you couldn't stomach the lunch you had this afternoon, I had our bus driver find us an afternoon snack that you might enjoy more. If some of you will help me hand these out. . . ."

Mrs. Waverly had managed to locate sack lunches containing ham and cheese sandwiches, oranges and chocolate bars for the entire group. After taking a bow to the round of applause she was given, she disappeared again into the front seat.

"She's great, isn't she?" Todd said as he dug for the candy bar in his sack lunch. "I was afraid we were going to have to last until supper on that awful salmon."

"She really is," Lexi agreed softly. "Ever since I moved to Cedar River I've felt like she's been really nice to me."

"That's the way she is. She's tough, but fair. Mom says the school system is lucky to have her."

Lexi nodded sleepily. That early morning alarm

was finally catching up with her. She yawned once, twice and a third time before she curled into a ball and rested her head against her arm. That was the last thing Lexi remembered until the bus pulled into the parking lot of the Plattstown Community Center.

"We're here."

"Where's here?"

"Plattstown."

"What's that?"

"That's where we have only thirty minutes until we're supposed to be giving a concert!"

That statement woke Lexi up quickly. The bus had pulled beside a rear door. Nearer the front of the building she could see concert-goers already arriving. They were coming to hear the Emerald Tones— little did they know that at the moment the Emerald Tones were a crazy mass of disorganization.

They piled out of the bus and into the locker rooms that had been designated as changing rooms. Out came the green jackets—this time looking a little less crisp than before.

Lexi stared at herself in a scratched, wavy mirror.

The mascara that she'd put on in Bernersville had come off her eyelashes and was lying on her cheeks in big, dark smudges. Her hair looked as rumpled as the white cotton blouse she was wearing. Near her ear, Jennifer groaned.

"I look like I was put together at the circus!"

"Welcome to the club," Lexi muttered. "How many minutes do we have to pull this together?" Going on tour was losing some of its glamour. In fact, it was beginning to seem like downright drudgery.

Still, they managed to pull it all together.

When they marched across the stage and onto the risers, and the crowd began to clap, even Lexi forgot the hours on the bus and the dreadful salmon loaf and all the times that the people in the back row had sung the same round over and over again.

When the final round of applause filled the auditorium, Lexi experienced an overwhelming feeling of satisfaction for a job well done.

"Great job, people!" Mrs. Waverly said with a beaming smile. Her beige hair was beginning to deflate a little and she looked tired—as tired as Lexi felt.

"There are host families waiting out front for you. They've graciously invited you to stay in their homes tonight. I'd like you all to be on your very best behavior. Each of you should take your bags and go into the gym and look for the family name I will give to you. Todd, you and Harry are staying with the Gundersons. Lonnie and Joe are with the McPhersons, Jennifer and Lexi must find the Tripplets. . . ."

"Tripplets! What a crazy name," Jennifer muttered. "There must be three of them. Or six. Or nine. Tripplets come in base three!"

"You're getting goofy," Lexi pointed out. "Let's just find our host family and get to bed. I can't even see straight any more."

"Bad sign. First your vision goes, then your brain. . . ."

It was midnight by the time Lexi and Jennifer finally sank into the cottony softness of the bed in the Tripplet's guest bedroom.

"I'm so tired my toes are numb," Jennifer complained as she snuggled down into the mattress and pulled the blankets a little higher over her head.

"Well, my legs are numb," Lexi retorted drowsily.

"And my arms. . . ."

"And my head. . . ."

"And my mouth. . . ." With that, Jennifer slipped off to sleep.

Lexi curled a little deeper into the blankets and allowed herself to drift into a deep, dreamless slumber.

Not even for a moment did she wonder how things were going at home or if her mother had solved whatever mysterious problem was making her so unhappy.

———

"How do musicians *do* it?" Jennifer wondered as she pressed her nose to the already smudged windows of the bus. "Touring day after day, week after week, month after month—"

"We get the picture, Jennifer," Todd interrupted. "You're tired."

"We've only been gone two days and it seems like at least a week!"

"It was fun though, wasn't it?" Lexi added, her eyes shining. "I think we were a real hit everywhere we sang."

"Yeah, and the food got better the second day."

"No more salmon loaf. . . ."

"And no more peas. . . ."

"And the school in Porter invited us back next year!"

It was after midnight when the bus finally pulled in at the Cedar River High School. Lexi and Jennifer waited until most everyone had filed off the bus before leaving their seats. Only Todd and Harry were behind them.

"Need a ride home, Harry?" Todd asked.

"Yeah. Great. Then I won't have to call my folks and tell them we've arrived."

"Look! My parents are here!" Lexi pointed out. "Jennifer, do you want a ride?"

"Nah. I think that's my dad just pulling up at the other end of the school."

"G'night, then. See you tomorrow in school."

Jennifer groaned. "They should call it off. Don't they realize how *tired* we'll be?"

"I have a hunch that we won't get much sympathy," Lexi pointed out. "After all, we've just skipped two days of school."

"Too true. Well, see you in class!" Jennifer hiked her bag onto her shoulder and started trudging toward her father's car.

Todd ruffled Lexi's hair with his hand. "Sleep fast, Lex. Morning is going to come early tomorrow. Come on, Harry, let's go."

"How's the Leighton family musician?" Lexi's father stood on the concrete with his fists propped on his hips. "Ready to go home or do you want a few more days on the road?"

"Home. Definitely home." Lexi threw her arms around her mother. "Where's Ben? Did you get a babysitter?"

"Are you kidding? Would Ben miss your big homecoming?" Mr. Leighton chuckled as he picked up Lexi's luggage. "He's asleep in the back seat of the car. He couldn't keep his eyes open two minutes."

It was true. Ben was snoring soundly in the back seat, his head thrown back, his pink little mouth wide open. Lexi had the urge to pick him up and give him a squeeze, but she resisted, knowing that if Ben were even *half* as tired as she, he needed his sleep.

"So tell us how it was," Mr. Leighton asked as he drove. "Did you 'wow' 'em?"

Lexi plunged wholeheartedly into every detail of the two day trip. It was not until they reached home that she realized that something had changed in the brief time since she had left.

"It sounds as though you had a marvelous time, Lexi," Mrs. Leighton was saying, her voice bright and lilting. "I'm delighted that the school is doing this for its students. Why, when I was in school. . . ."

Lexi stared at her mother. What had happened? When she'd left, her mom was . . . Lexi searched her mind for a word . . . gloomy. Now she was bubbling with excitement over Lexi's trip, laughing and clapping her hands.

Lexi stared at her for a long moment. Finally she mustered up the courage to ask, "What's up, Mom?"

Mrs. Leighton blinked. "What do you mean?"

"You're acting . . . different. Happy. Like you've got a great big, special secret or something."

Mr. and Mrs. Leighton exchanged a look.

"You're very astute, Lexi, we do have a secret, sort of. Actually, it's a surprise."

"A surprise? So, tell me! What is it?"

They were just pulling into the garage. As the car

went over the bump in the curb, Ben snuffled and woke up.

"Lexi's home!"

"Hiya, Ben. Why don't you go back to sleep and say hello to me in the morning?"

Ben gave her a sleepy look and then snuggled back into the seat. "Okay."

Mr. Leighton parked the car and came to lift Ben from the back seat. Lexi carried her bag and Mrs. Leighton followed behind switching off lights and shutting doors.

"I think I'll go to bed too," Lexi said with a yawn. "I'm as sleepy as Ben."

"Good idea. We'll talk in the morning."

Lexi was already in bed, her teeth brushed and her lights out when she realized that she still didn't know what her mother's "surprise" might be.

Chapter Four

Morning came far too early the next day, Lexi decided, as she hurried to get ready for school. She had punched the snooze bar on her alarm clock three times before she decided she had to get up. Ben was sleepily spooning cereal into his mouth when Lexi came downstairs.

"Good morning, Ben," she said.

"Hi, Lexi." His dark eyes brightened.

Lexi gave him a squeeze. "You were asleep last night when I got home from the tour."

Ben's lips turned down in a frown. "Ben was sleepy."

"I know exactly how you feel," Lexi commiserated. "I'm sleepy this morning."

Just then, Mr. Leighton entered the kitchen. "Good morning, kids," he said cheerfully. "Did I hear someone say they were tired?"

Lexi gave a yawn. "Too many late nights, Dad."

Her father smiled. "I hope they aren't so many that you've forgotten what you promised to do after school today."

Lexi's eyebrows knit in a frown. "What was that, Dad?"

"Today you were going to come to my office and learn the ropes of your new job."

Lexi snapped her fingers. "Right! How could I forget? I'll come as soon as school is out."

Mr. Leighton nodded. "Good. My secretary's son came down with the chicken pox yesterday and I know that she'd like to get home as early as she could. Perhaps you could answer the phone for her for a couple of hours."

"Sure, Dad. Anything you want."

Just then, Mrs. Leighton came bustling into the kitchen. "I don't know what you two are talking about, but I think you'd better finish your conversation in the car. Have you looked at the time?" Her gaze fell on the clock on the wall.

Lexi's eyes traveled the same path. "Almost eight-fifteen!" she yelped. "Can you give me a ride, Dad?"

Her father nodded and Lexi grabbed her school bag and headed for the car. He'd dropped her off at the front door of Cedar River High and waved his goodbye before Lexi remembered the one thing she had wanted to discuss with her parents this morning. In all the rush to get ready and the conversation about starting her new job at the veterinary clinic, Lexi had forgotten to ask about the surprise her mother had mentioned the night before.

"Oh well," Lexi said to herself and gave a little shrug. Any surprise that made her mother seem that happy was bound to be a good one. She would find out tonight what had brought the smile back to her mother's face.

"It is *so* radical, you will not believe it! You will simply not believe it!" Minda was holding court at the far end of the hallway. A group of girls, including several members of the High-Five Club, were standing in a semi-circle looking at Minda in awe and admiration.

"Now what's up?" Lexi asked Jennifer, as they exchanged books in their locker between classes.

"Minda just got a new stereo system," Jennifer informed her. "She's telling everyone what a great sound it has."

"A new stereo system? Her old one can't be more than a year or two old."

Jennifer shrugged. "You know Minda. When something new comes out, she has to have it right away. Her dad bought it for her." Jennifer's eyes narrowed. "Minda's parents still haven't reconciled. Sometimes I think that Minda's father is trying to buy her affection or loyalty by giving her all of these things."

Lexi was silent. She didn't really like Minda, but she did feel sorry for her. Minda's parents were separated and her mother drank too much.

Lexi knew that no matter how many new stereos or how many new outfits Minda received, she would never trade places with her. Her family, especially the wonderful relationship she had with her parents, was too important for that. Minda's father worked long hours and she seldom saw him. Minda's mother spent her time drinking cocktails and playing bridge at the country club.

Lexi gave a little inward shudder at the thought. No, no matter what Minda had, Lexi wouldn't trade her for it. The relationship she had with her own mother was far too important.

"What are you thinking about?" Jennifer inquired bluntly. "Minda and her new stereo system?"

Lexi shook her head. "Actually, I was thinking about my mom. I've been so busy that it's been a long time since we've done anything together, like go shopping or have lunch, you know?"

Jennifer nodded. "Yeah, my mom and I are going out to the mall on Saturday. We both need new shoes."

Lexi smiled. "Actually, that sounds like a good idea—a shopping trip with my mom. She's been talking about trying the spinach salad at Samuels. Maybe I'll ask Mom if that's what she wants to do on Saturday."

"Whatever. All I know is that if we don't hurry, we're going to be late for class."

Lexi nodded briskly and followed her friend down the hallway. She was feeling good about her decision. It was time to have some fun with her mother. Smiling, Lexi went to class.

———

Todd was waiting for her at the end of the day. He was leaning against the doorjamb, tapping his foot and whistling.

"Hi," Lexi greeted him. "Any special reason you're standing here like a lamppost?"

Todd grinned. "Want a ride to the veterinary

clinic? Or isn't this the day that you're supposed to start your new job?"

Lexi nodded. "I'm glad you remembered. I almost forgot. My dad had to remind me this morning."

"I never forget anything about you, Lexi. You should know that by now," Todd pointed out with a playful grin.

A rush of warmth flooded through Lexi. She loved it when Todd said things like that. Todd knew how to make her feel special, with a smile or a look or a word. Lexi threw her school bag into the back seat of the '49 Ford and crawled into the front. She enjoyed riding around in the old car, just as much as Todd loved to drive it. He kept it polished to a high gloss and the interior vacuumed until it was spotless. He had a little pine tree air freshener hanging from the rear view mirror and a country western station playing on the radio.

"Do you have time for something to eat first?" he wondered.

Lexi shook her head. "I'd better not. Dad's secretary wants to leave early today."

"So you haven't even started yet and you've already been promoted to secretary?" Todd grinned. "Pretty impressive."

"And I'll be demoted again when the secretary's child recovers from the chicken pox."

"I know how that goes. I'm always 'in charge' of my brother Mike's garage when he has to go to the bank or get the mail, but as soon as he comes back, I'm back to my old job as second fiddle."

Lexi nodded. "I think that's about what I'm going to be. I hope Dad has some interesting animals in the cages that will be fun to take care of."

"I've never been in your Dad's veterinary clinic," Todd pointed out. "Would you mind giving me a tour?"

They were pulling up in front of the light brick building with brown shake roof and dark brown shutters.

"Looks like a nice place."

"It is. Come on inside. If it's not too busy, I'll take you back and show you where Dad keeps his patients."

Just inside the doorway, their senses were assaulted with the smells of antiseptics and pet food. In the foyer of the clinic was a row of pale grey chairs lining light mauve walls. The kind of music that Lexi liked to call "elevator music" was playing softly from hidden speakers.

Todd looked around. "Hey! This looks like a real doctor's office."

"My dad is a real doctor," Lexi explained.

"You know what I mean. A real people doctor."

Lexi pointed to the bags of pet food stacked on shelves in one corner. "I suppose there are some differences in my dad's patients than other doctors'."

A lady in a bright blue dress was seated on one of the chairs. In her lap she held a tiny brown and white Chihuahua dog. When Todd and Lexi walked through the door, the dog started to yap at the top of its tiny lungs.

"Quiet, Muffy. Quiet, darling. Be a good baby, Muffy. Don't bark at the nice people. Quiet, Muffy. Shhh, baby . . ."

Todd and Lexi exchanged a quick, amused glance.

The lady was holding the Chihuahua like it was an infant—cradling it in her arms and crooning into its little brown ear. "Don't be scared, Muffy. Everything's fine. You're just going to have a little shot and we'll take you out of here. Would Muffy like ice cream?"

Todd's eyes grew round and Lexi covered her mouth to hide a smile. She was more used to seeing people treat their pets like children than Todd was. Once a lady had brought her Pekingese to the clinic in Grover's Point wrapped in a white lace baby blanket and drinking from a baby bottle.

Lexi's father said that sometimes if people didn't have children or others close to them, they turned all the love and emotion they had toward their pets. Lexi looked again to the lady in the bright blue dress and the little Chihuahua—which she was now feeding doggy biscuits from her pocket—and didn't doubt for a moment that her father was right.

"Lexi. Is that you?"

"Hello, Mrs. Harmon. Are you waiting to go home? I can take over for you now."

Lexi walked up to the receptionist's desk and leaned over the counter.

"That would be wonderful," Mrs. Harmon said. "I left my little boy with a sitter, but neither of them were too happy about it. He's just breaking out and very itchy."

"Well, show me what to do," Lexi said as she stepped around the desk.

"Just answer the phone by saying 'Leighton Veterinary Clinic, how may I help you?' and take whatever message the caller has. If someone would like to make an appointment, just fill it in in the book here." Mrs. Harmon tapped on the open appointment book. "It's fairly clear what hours your father has free. If you have a question about how long a procedure will take, just step in the back and ask your father."

Mrs. Harmon showed Lexi how to use the telephone system and how to put a caller on hold. She explained the abbreviations that she used in the appointment book. Then she gathered up her purse and jacket.

"Thanks for helping out, Lexi. I buzzed your dad when you came and told him you were here. He'll be out as soon as he's free."

"Is it all right if I take Todd on a little tour of the back rooms?" Lexi asked.

Mrs. Harmon glanced at the nearly empty waiting room. "I suppose. Just keep your ears open in case someone else comes in."

After she'd gone, Lexi led Todd into the first small room behind the secretary's desk. "This is where they keep medicines and salves," Lexi said as she pointed to the shelves lined with small bottles and tubes. "This means if your cat needs an antibiotic, you can get it right here." She held up a little blue bottle with a green and white label. "This one works something like penicillin. Dad explained it to me."

Todd nodded as he took in his surroundings. "Very impressive."

Lexi waved him on. "Come and see the examining rooms."

They walked down a long hallway lined on both sides with pictures of purebred pets. There were photos of a black lab, a golden retriever, a white and black spotted Dalmatian and even a wrinkled Sharpei.

"Dad must be in the first examining room," Lexi noted, "so we'll go into this one." She turned into an antiseptic-looking white room with a metal table and bright lights.

"Wow!" Todd said. "This looks like an operating room."

"Dad says it's very important to keep everything sanitary," Lexi said, but Todd was not listening. He was busy examining a beige colored canvas bag with a heavy duty zipper up one side.

"What's this?" he wondered.

"That's for holding a cat," Lexi explained.

"A cat?"

"For example, if you wanted to examine a cat for ear mites, but the cat is frightened and might scratch and claw, you can put it in a bag like that, so only its head sticks out. Then it can't go anywhere or scratch you. They don't like it," Lexi chuckled, "but it doesn't hurt them and no one gets scratched."

"Interesting," Todd said. "You know, I've thought about going into medicine, but I never really thought about *veterinary* medicine until today."

"Come on out back. Dad has a place for larger animals as well, even though his specialty is small pets." Lexi showed him the dog room, the cat room and even the bird room, and then they walked all the way to the back where there were stalls for even larger animals.

"You could keep a horse in here," Todd pointed out.

Lexi nodded. "Or at the very least, a Saint Bernard."

They were peering into one of the big cages when Lexi's father's voice came floating through the air to them. "Lexi? Are you back here?"

"Hi, Dad. I was just showing Todd the clinic."

"Would you like to call my last patient? I believe it's a Chihuahua with the sniffles."

Lexi grinned at Todd and hurried to the front of the office. She sent the lady in the bright blue dress and her dog to the free examining room, answered the telephone and received a package from the delivery man.

Todd wandered out from back of the clinic. "Looks like you're plenty busy without having me here to bother you, Lexi," he said. "I think I'll just go home. Thanks for the tour."

"Sure, anytime. Thanks for the ride."

He waved at her as he pulled out of the parking lot. Lexi stepped to the window and waved back. Just then, a fury of barking started in the dog room. Lexi's father stuck his head out of the examining room door. "I think the natives are getting restless, Lexi. Would you like to feed the dogs? You know where the food is, don't you?"

Lexi nodded briskly and headed for the large, white plastic canisters on the floor of the dog room. She measured out scoops of food into each of the dishes and then took a long-nosed pitcher and filled each of the water dishes.

There were two cats confined in the other room. Lexi rummaged in the small refrigerator until she found a can of cat food. She measured the cat food into the bowls and was rewarded with the sounds of their loud, rumbling purrrr. "You guys must be getting better," she said to the cats, a grey and white tabby and a sleek Siamese. "Your appetites are good."

Just then, her father joined her. "How are you doing on your first day at work? I'm sorry Mrs. Harmon had to leave in such a hurry. She didn't have time to give you many directions."

Lexi grinned. "It's all right. I remember doing these things for you in Grover's Point."

"Did you show Todd the exotic pet room?"

Lexi shook her head. "I forgot. Is anything in there?"

"Well, we have two ferrets and a parrot at the moment. You should have come two days ago. I had a boa constrictor with a tummy ache."

Lexi wrinkled her nose. "I'm glad I missed that, Dad. I fed the dogs and the cats, but I'm not sure what to do about the ferrets or a parrot."

Her father had just finished giving instructions when a bell rang, signaling that someone had entered the front door.

"I'll go get it," Lexi volunteered. "If I'm going to fill in for your secretary, I might as well start right now." Lexi wound her way back to the front of the building to find Chad Allen standing at the reception desk. He was straining to hold a rather fierce looking Doberman at the end of a leash.

"Chad!" Lexi gasped.

Chad blinked as if he were surprised to see her. "What are you doing here, Lexi?" he wondered.

"This is my dad's office. Who's this?" Lexi stared at the Doberman.

"This is Waldo," Chad said with an apologetic

grin. "Your dad's been treating him for a cut on his leg that got infected."

"Hello, Chad. Hello, Waldo," said Lexi's father from over Lexi's shoulder.

"Hello, Dr. Leighton," Chad said politely.

Now it was Lexi's turn to be startled. She wasn't used to hearing her father called "Dr. Leighton." Especially by her friends.

Chad and Waldo disappeared into the examining room with Lexi's father, and she was left to straighten up the magazines in the waiting room and make an appointment for someone with an ailing cockapoo. It wasn't long until Chad and the Doberman returned to the lobby.

"How's Waldo?" Lexi asked politely.

"Fine, thanks to your dad," Chad answered. Though the Doberman was pulling eagerly on its leash, Chad seemed in no hurry to follow him. He hesitated a moment as if to muster his courage before asking, "Have you heard from Peggy lately, Lexi?"

Lexi cast her eyes downward. Chad was Peggy's boyfriend. He was the father of the baby Peggy had gone to Arizona to have, and Chad was asking *her* if she had heard from Peggy lately? "Last week," Lexi finally murmured. "Why?"

Chad shrugged. "Just wondering. She hasn't exactly written to me a lot." He hesitated and an unhappy expression washed over his features. "She says she's pretty . . . mixed up."

"So she's not writing to you?"

Chad shook his head. "Sometimes she writes to say she can hardly wait to get home to see me. Other times, she thinks we should be breaking up."

Lexi gave him a compassionate look. "Give her time, Chad. That's part of why she went away—so that she could have some help with her emotions. Her uncle is a doctor. He'll know what to do."

Chad gave a discouraged sigh. "We really blew it, Peggy and I. We had no business messing around like we did. Now we've brought another person—a baby—into this world." His voice wavered and Lexi could tell that his emotions were very near the surface.

There was nothing for Lexi to say. She agreed completely with Chad. He and Peggy *had* messed up and now they were paying the price.

Chad shuffled uncomfortably from one foot to the other. In the meantime, the big dog pulled on its leash. "Well, I guess I'd better be going," he finally stammered.

"Chad," Lexi began. He looked at her hopefully. "When I write to Peggy, I'll tell her we talked."

He nodded. "Thanks, I'd like that. Maybe it'll help."

Lexi was thoughtful after Chad left. Why was everything always so complicated? Why couldn't things be simple and straightforward? Then she smiled. At least they were simple and straightforward at her house. *Wouldn't it be wonderful,* Lexi thought, *if everyone could have a family as great as hers?*

"It's almost five-thirty, Lexi," her father said as he came out of the back shrugging out of his white doctor's coat. "Time to go home."

"I haven't fed the rest of the animals."

"Never mind. I took care of it," he said cheerfully. "You've helped out enough for one day. Thank you. Now let's go home and see what your mother has on the stove for supper."

Lexi closed her eyes and listened to the music playing on the car radio as her father drove toward home. There was something that she had meant to ask him. Something she wanted to talk about. Lexi knew, but she couldn't quite remember what it was. Something about last night. When they'd been driving home from the school. What was it she had meant to ask her father?

Their minds must have been traveling along the same path, because just then, Mr. Leighton turned toward Lexi and said, "Lexi, honey, there's something that I wanted to talk to you about before we got home."

"Yeah, Dad?" Lexi said, puzzled. Her father normally didn't look quite so serious.

"It's about what we were discussing last night."

Lexi snapped her fingers as she remembered. "That's it. That's it, Dad. I wanted to ask you about this 'surprise' Mom was talking about last night."

A frown flitted across Mr. Leighton's features. "Well, Lexi, I wanted to warn you that your mother *does* have something up her sleeve. I wanted her to think this through a little more and to discuss it with you before she went ahead, but—"

"Dad! Look out!" Lexi screamed.

Suddenly, a car seemed to be coming at them from out of nowhere. Instinctively, Lexi raised her hands over her head and squeezed her eyes shut tight. Mr. Leighton moved his foot from the gas peddle to the brake and she could hear the squealing of tires and a whimper that she realized later must have been her own. But there was no crash, no grinding of metal, no shattering of glass. Hesitantly, Lexi lowered her arms from over her face. Her father was leaning with his forehead against the steering wheel. His hands, white knuckled, still clenched tightly about the wheel.

"That was close," he breathed. "We can thank God for watching over us that time."

"What happened?" Lexi said in a quavering voice.

"That car," and Mr. Leighton pointed toward the red sports car that hardly seemed more than a speck on the horizon now, "nearly sideswiped us."

"He didn't even stop!"

Mr. Leighton shook his head. "That kind never does. Reckless drivers not only don't care about their own lives, but they obviously don't care about the lives of others on the highways around them."

They were both very shaken and finished the rest of the drive home in silence.

It wasn't until Mrs. Leighton met Lexi and her father at the kitchen door that Lexi recalled the conversation she and her father had been having just prior to their near accident. Some of her father's words came back to her. "I wanted your mother to think this over more first. She should have talked to you."

Somehow now, after their recent car episode, the words had taken on an ominous ring. What was it that Mrs. Leighton should have talked over with Lexi? What was it that Lexi's own father did not feel quite comfortable about? Lexi stared for a long moment at her mother.

Something wasn't right and Lexi knew whatever it was had to do with her mother and the "secret" that she had been unwilling to discuss last night.

Chapter Five

"Come in! Supper is all ready. I made something special and we'll have to eat right away or it will be ruined!" Mrs. Leighton ushered Lexi and her father into the dining room where Ben was already seated at the table.

Lexi couldn't remember her mother being this excited about a meal in a long time. "This looks great!" Lexi gasped as she stared at the table.

Mrs. Leighton had used the crystal she and Lexi's father had received as wedding presents and great Grandma Leighton's Haviland china. There were cloth napkins at each place and tiny crystal salt cellars with miniature silver spoons with every setting. Even Lexi's father whistled low under his breath at the sight.

"Very impressive, Marilyn."

"Thanks. Now sit down, kids. Jim, you too. The popovers will be done in two minutes and they have to be served straight from the oven."

"Popovers!" Ben yelped. "Yum."

Lexi glanced uneasily about the room. Things

were just too . . . perfect. She was accustomed to having things a little more disorganized around here. Usually they were eating supper to the smells of turpentine and oil paints, not potpourri and freshly baked popovers.

Then Lexi shrugged. Her imagination was going wild. That was probably from lack of rest. Tomorrow the household—and her mind—would be back to normal. Tonight she'd just have to enjoy the party her mother had planned for their family.

"Marilyn, will you ask the blessing?"

Lexi's mom nodded and folded her hands. As Lexi bowed her head, she noticed the intense expression on her mother's face.

"Dear Father," she began, "tonight I ask your blessing on this food we are about to receive. Thank you for the daily gifts you shower upon us, for Lexi's safe return from the tour, for the marvelous gift of family. Today especially, Lord, I ask for the understanding and support of my children. May Ben and Lexi realize that the gifts you've given us are meant to be shared, not selfishly hoarded. . . ."

Lexi stiffened. This was not the usual sort of grace her mother asked before meals.

" . . . and bless us all in the work we are about to undertake. Amen."

"Amen!" Ben echoed and reached for his napkin.

Lexi was not quite so enthusiastic.

"What did you mean, Mom?"

"Mean?" Mrs. Leighton didn't do a very good job at looking innocent.

Lexi had a queasy, uncomfortable sensation in the pit of her stomach. She was beginning to feel as if she'd already eaten—and it wasn't digesting very well. She shifted uneasily on the chair.

Ben laid down his fork and stared at Lexi. Lexi's discomfort seemed to have even her little brother worried. A shallow furrow of a frown marked the little boy's smooth forehead.

Mrs. Leighton smiled brightly and placed her napkin next to her plate. "The popovers! I almost forgot them!" She pushed away from the table and disappeared into the kitchen.

Lexi stared at her father but he refused to look up from his plate. When he did, his eyes were troubled.

"Your mom wanted to surprise you with this, Lexi. I didn't think it was a good idea, but it all happened so fast . . . while you were on tour. . . ."

"Here they are!" Mrs. Leighton came in bearing a plate of steaming popovers. Suddenly, they didn't seem so appealing.

"What's going on, Mom? Dad? What's the big 'surprise' that you concocted while I was gone? Why is it some big secret?"

Mrs. Leighton placed the plate on the table and sat down. She folded her hands and cradled her chin on the tops of her fingers. "It's not a secret, Lexi. I'm hoping this will be a surprise—a pleasant one. I know I'm very excited."

So come on, Mom, tell me what it is!

"Lexi, I've applied to become a foster parent."

There was a long, suspenseful pause that swelled until it filled the room and started to choke Lexi.

"A foster parent?"

Mrs. Leighton nodded. "Isn't that a wonderful idea?"

"But what about *us*?"

"Us," Ben echoed, still not comprehending the conversation. "Us."

Mrs. Leighton looked puzzled. "What do you mean, Lexi?"

"I mean, *why*? Aren't Ben and I enough kids for you? You need more?"

Mrs. Leighton's hands fluttered helplessly in the air. "Lexi! What a thing to say!" Then a determined expression settled on her features.

"You and Ben have settled beautifully into life in Cedar River. Ben is progressing faster than we ever anticipated at the Academy for the Handicapped. You're active in the school, you've made friends, your grade point is high, you've even started to work for your father."

"So?" Lexi asked stubbornly. There was a tight, angry feeling in her mid-section that simply wouldn't go away. A foster parent? What was wrong with the kids her parents already had?

"My painting is a wonderful hobby, Lexi. I love doing the art shows and will continue to do them. And there's nothing more heady than having someone actually *buy* one of my pictures—"

"So why do you need to do more?"

Mrs. Leighton ran her fingers through her hair in a frustrated gesture, but Lexi doubted that her mother could be any more frustrated than she herself felt right now.

"Painting isn't enough, honey. It's a hobby, not a career."

"But—"

"Lexi, I've felt ever since the day you were born

that God had a plan for me, that He'd given me some very special talents."

"Sure, Mom, but—"

"No, hear me out. Let me tell you about my talents."

Lexi fell silent.

"He gave me the skills of nurturing and mothering, Lexi. He gave me patience and love and concern. I needed all of those when you were a baby and especially when Ben came along. Every one of God's gifts got put to use when we found out that Ben was retarded. My patience—even my faith—was stretched to the limit. But you know what I discovered?"

Ben was staring at his mother, his little pink mouth open.

"I discovered that loving a baby with a handicap is just as easy and rewarding and fulfilling as loving any other kind. A 'challenge baby.' That's what the doctor called Ben. And, you know what? We all lived up to the challenge."

"But that was *Ben*. He's ours."

"I'm yours," Ben agreed.

"And now Ben is growing up to be a self-sufficient little boy. The school says that someday Ben will be able to live in a group home and have a job."

"I'm too little!" Ben complained, worried that he was going to be put into the work force immediately.

"Not now, honey. When you're a man."

"Oh." Ben turned back to his popover. "Ben's a boy now."

"I still don't understand. Ben *is* just a boy. He still needs you. *I* still need you!"

"And you'll have me!" Mrs. Leighton leaned across the table. "You have to understand, Lexi, that I believe God is calling me to do this—to have foster children. Now that you and Ben are growing up so beautifully, He's calling me to use those talents He's given me for some other child. I've got plenty of love to go around, Lexi. More than you can imagine. It doesn't mean there will be less love for you if we take in a foster child. It may mean there'll be more."

"More?"

"Wouldn't you like a sister to share with, Lexi?"

"I might have when I was little, but now it's . . . too late."

"It's never too late to find someone to love."

"But it's too late to pretend that someone is my sister!"

Lexi's words were harsh and angry. How could her mother do this to her? She and Ben weren't all that grown up and independent! It was just her mother worrying about becoming useless or something weird like that. She and Ben needed their mother—*all of her*!

"Maybe you should explain to Lexi how this all came about," Mr. Leighton murmured. He'd been silent until now, wearing a troubled expression on his face. "After all, it's come as quite a shock—to all of us."

Mrs. Leighton nodded. "Frankly, it's been a surprise to me, too. I really didn't intend for any of this to happen." She looked somberly at Lexi. "That's why I'm sure God's hand is in all of this. Sometimes, when you least expect it, He gives you a nudge in a new direction."

Lexi stared doubtfully at her mother. Granted, she *had* prayed that God would help her mother, but she certainly hadn't expected anything like this!

"I was at the church working on Sunday school material one afternoon when Pastor introduced me to a woman named Anna McNeil. Anna works for the Children and Family Services Division of the Department of Human Services. She was at the church to acquaint people with her department and let them know what a great need there was for foster parents."

"What's foster parents?" Ben demanded. He was the only one who'd managed to eat any of his food. The rest of his family was too caught up in the intense conversation.

"Foster parents are people who take children into their homes when the children can't stay in their own homes."

Ben blinked. Lexi knew he couldn't comprehend why any child would have to leave his own home.

"Foster parents treat these children just like their own. They give them food and clothing, love and discipline—just like Dad and I give to you."

Ben looked blankly at his mother.

"Not everybody is as lucky as you, Ben. Sometimes a mom or dad can't take care of their own kids like they'd like to. Sometimes they need time to get themselves together, to get a new job, to get counselling. That's when foster parents can help out."

"But why you?" Lexi protested. All this information was fine and dandy—but why couldn't it be someone else's parents?

"Because we can do everything that foster parents need to be able to do. We can offer a child all the physical necessities and things like love, stability and guidance as well. Sometimes foster kids are kids who have run away from home because they're so unhappy in their own homes. We can show them what a happy home is like."

A formerly happy home, Lexi thought sourly.

"Anyway, Anna McNeil encouraged me to look into the program. She gave me the application for licensure and I filled it out and didn't think much more about it." Mrs. Leighton turned to Lexi. "I forgot about it—until two days ago."

"After we went on tour?"

Mrs. Leighton nodded. "I received a phone call that morning from Social Services. They'd checked out the application and the references. They were calling to do a fire and safety check of our house."

"Our house is safe!" Lexi protested indignantly.

"Of course it is, but they wanted to see that for themselves."

"So what was the big hurry?"

Mrs. Leighton glanced at her husband. "Apparently a big need has recently come up for adolescent foster care."

"What's adolescent?" Ben stammered over the long word.

"Teenagers," Lexi snapped sharply. "Like me."

"Anna says that more families are willing to take younger children than older ones. When there's suddenly a big demand for homes for teens they sometimes have to scramble to find them."

"And they asked you to do it," Lexi concluded. Her stomach hurt and she felt a prickly, scratchy feeling behind her eyes. Even her throat felt hot and tight.

"Think about it, Lexi! Wouldn't it be wonderful to know you were helping some needy teenager— someone who didn't have a home to go to right now? Wouldn't it feel marvelous to know that you were helping someone who needed it so much?"

Lexi glanced doubtfully at her mother. Maybe that's how her mother felt, but it certainly wasn't the way Lexi felt! She had enough trouble with teenagers at school—Minda Hannaford, for one. Minda had a crummy homelife and she took it out on everyone around her. How could someone who'd been forced to leave their home be any better?

Mrs. Leighton was still talking, trying to convince Lexi of the rightness of her decision.

"I know this is the right thing to do, Lexi. I've prayed about it a great deal in the past two days. It's right. It's what I should be doing. I'm sure of it."

"You too, Dad?" Lexi turned to her father.

His face was furrowed with concern. "I believe your mother would be excellent, Lexi. And I love children—you know that. But we need your cooperation, too."

Lexi pushed her chair away from the table. The harsh grating sound echoed in her ears as unpleasantly as her mother's words. "Excuse me, please. I think I need to think about this."

"Lexi, your dinner."

"I'm not hungry anymore, Mom. Thanks."

"But . . ."

Lexi didn't wait to hear what her mother said. Instead she rushed full tilt to her bedroom and closed and locked the door. She flung herself across the bed and clamped her hands over her ears wishing she could block out words that had already been spoken.

She didn't want to share her house or her parents or her life with a stranger! She didn't want someone coming here and taking up her parents' time and energy! She wanted things to remain as they were. She pounded furiously at the feather pillow on her bed. Already she disliked this faceless, nameless intruder who was going to come to their house and wreck her life.

She lay there a long time.

She could hear her parents washing the dishes and cleaning up the kitchen. Ben took his bath and padded by her bedroom on his way to bed.

He whispered a tiny " 'Night, Lexi" outside her door.

Finally, she heard her parents mount the stairs and enter their bedroom.

She hated the idea of a foster child! She *hated* it. But what she hated more was this awful feeling of guilt building up inside her.

As Lexi lay on the bed staring around at her room, her gaze fell on her stereo system, the open door to her closet filled with clothes, her desk and the corkboard filled with photos of family vacations.

She did have it awfully nice, Lexi mused. Maybe that was why she didn't want to share it with any strangers. This was *her* room. *Her* things.

Still, the guilt grew.

Lexi flip-flopped on the bed.

She *had* been pretty lucky in her life.

Was it selfish not to want to share that?

She knew how much her parents loved her and Ben. She didn't doubt that for a minute.

So why should she be worried about having another person come and stay at the house for a few days or weeks?

How bad could it be?

Pretty bad said a voice in her head.

She stared at the ceiling for a long time before pulling herself up to reach for the book on the bedside stand.

Whenever she had a problem she couldn't solve, Lexi always went to the Bible. Her parents had taught her that. Sometimes when things were just too much of a jumble for her to make sense of them, a verse or two of Scripture could put everything in perspective.

Not even knowing where to begin looking for guidance, Lexi allowed the Book to fall open.

Exodus.

Lexi felt a twinge of surprise. Usually she liked to read in the New Testament. It seemed so much more modern to her somehow, easier to understand. Still, she began to read.

In the twentieth chapter, she found the Ten Commandments. She skimmed the words, not knowing what she was looking for. Then one verse leapt out at her.

"Honor your father and your mother. . . ."

It was as clear and sharp as a bolt of lightning.

Honor your father and your mother.

Honor their decisions.

Even if you don't agree with them, because they are your parents, you must honor them.

Lexi closed the Book gently.

Well, she thought to herself. She had her answer. If her mother and father wanted to go through with the foster parent thing, then she'd go along with it— to honor them.

Still, Lexi mused as she turned out the light and stared into a room filled with darkness, it was hard. Doing the right thing wasn't always easy. She still had this miserable feeling in her stomach that wouldn't go away.

She would tell her parents in the morning that whatever they decided was acceptable to her.

Lexi burrowed deeply beneath her covers in an attempt to close out the thoughts that kept creeping in to haunt her.

Maybe this foster kid thing was *right* for her mother, but Lexi had the horrible feeling that it was going to be terribly *wrong* for her!

Chapter Six

"Good morning, Lexi." Mrs. Leighton stared uncertainly at her daughter.

"Hi, Mom."

"Lexi, about last night . . ."

"I'm sorry about that," Lexi murmured. "I guess I overreacted."

Mrs. Leighton nodded. "Perhaps. But it wasn't fair to spring this on you so suddenly, either. I didn't realize how upset you'd be. I assumed you'd *like* to help—"

"I would, Mom, really. It's just that it was pretty unexpected, that's all."

Mrs. Leighton smiled and laid a hand on Lexi's cheek. "You've always been the one to bring home a child who was having trouble making friends or an animal that looked like it hadn't been fed. I just expected you to jump into this with as much enthusiasm."

"I'm getting used to the idea, Mom. Really. I guess it's pretty selfish to not want to share you—"

"But you won't have to share me! I've got plenty

of love to go around!" Mrs. Leighton wrapped her arms around Lexi. "One thing about love, Lexi, is that the way to get more of it is to give it away. If you take love and hoard it and refuse to share it, it seems to whither and die. But if you give it away, more and more comes back to you. Trust me, you'll see."

Lexi nodded numbly. *Trust me.* She'd have to trust her mother on this one because it didn't feel like a good idea at all to her. It felt terrible to think of another person barging in on her territory, her *home!*

———

Lexi didn't even see Binky in the hallway at school until Binky stood right in front of her and demanded, "What's wrong with you today anyway? Can't you even say hello?"

"Oh, hi, Bink."

"Didn't you see me? I'm short, but not that short!"

"I've had a lot on my mind today, that's all."

"I guess so. I've seen you in class and in the hall-ways and you haven't even blinked. I even heard Minda tell someone you looked like you were in a daze."

Lexi wiped her hands across her eyes. "I guess I must be. I just about flunked a history quiz last hour and Mrs. Waverly had to tell me to pay attention in chorus."

"You're kidding!" Binky looked fisheyed with surprise. "The 'perfect' Lexi Leighton in trouble? What's going on?"

Lexi wanted to tell her, she really did, but she

just couldn't bring herself to talk about it. Not yet. Not until she got used to the idea herself. When she talked about her mom and dad becoming foster parents, she wanted to sound happy about it, like it was a good idea. She couldn't do that today.

Lexi swallowed thickly. She hoped she could sound happy about it sometime in this century.

———

"Ride?" Todd wondered after school as he leaned out of his '49 Ford, "or are you getting your exercise tonight?"

"Thanks, but I'll walk. I had a lousy day today. I need to think." Lexi gave him a weak excuse for a smile.

Todd nodded compassionately. He'd seen Mrs. Waverly scold Lexi for not paying attention. "Okay. If you want to talk later, I'll be at my brother Mike's garage. I told Matt Windsor that I'd help him work on his motorcycle."

Lexi nodded and waved as Todd drove away. She was grateful for his understanding. He always seemed to sense when she needed to be alone and when she wanted company. He never pressed her to do anything she didn't want to do. Todd was very mature for his age.

A tear formed on the inside of her lower eyelid and Lexi brushed it away. Why couldn't *she* be mature about this? Why couldn't she feel good that her mother was so happy and excited about the foster parent program?

Feeling angry and guilty and miserable, Lexi stomped up the front steps and into her house.

A lady in a navy blue suit and grey pumps and blouse was sitting on the couch drinking coffee.

Lexi skidded to a halt in the hallway.

"Lexi? Come into the living room and meet Mrs. McNeil," her mother called.

Lexi swallowed twice before willing her feet to take her into the living room.

"So this is Lexi!" Mrs. McNeil said pleasantly. "How lovely you are, Lexi."

"Thank you."

"Want a cookie, Lexi? Some lemonade?"

"No thanks."

"The fire and safety checks on the house are all acceptable, isn't that great, dear?" Mrs. Leighton enthused. "Good news, right?"

"It was safe enough for us before."

"Of course it was, but Social Services doesn't know that so they have to come out and do a special check, that's all."

"What if they'd found something wrong?" Lexi wondered. "Then what?"

"Then we would have had it fixed."

"Would we have had it fixed if it were just our family living here?"

"We wouldn't have had the check-up, of course, so we might not have known. . . ."

"So our house has to be safer for a foster kid than it does for your own kids?"

Mrs. Leighton looked startled, as if she hadn't thought about it quite that way before.

Mrs. McNeil hurried to ask a question before the conversation could go any farther.

"How do you feel about your parents entering this program, Lexi?"

Lexi stared at the toes of her shoes. "It makes my mom very happy. She's excited."

"And how do *you* feel?"

"She's a really good mother. She'll be great."

"Well, that's high praise!" Mrs. McNeil said. Mrs. Leighton beamed.

Lexi had to answer a few more questions before she could escape to her bedroom to throw herself down on her bed.

What a terrible day this had been!

She'd nearly flunked a test.

Mrs. Waverly had scolded her.

Binky had been disgusted with her for being so self-absorbed.

Even Todd had looked a little bewildered when she refused his offer of a ride.

Still, she hadn't dared mention this scheme of her mother's to anyone, to explain why she was so upset.

And now Mrs. McNeil was sitting in the living room drinking coffee.

Lexi put her hands to her eyes and groaned. If only she had someone to talk to about this!

Lexi sat up and stared at herself in the mirror. But who would understand? She would sound so . . . selfish . . . wouldn't she? Wasn't that what this was all about? Being selfish and feeling guilty about it?

Lexi's shoulders sagged. That was it in a nutshell. She was feeling guilty because she didn't want a foster kid in the house. Where was her faith right now? If it had been Binky or Minda or anyone else in her shoes, Lexi would have told them to be big about it, to share their lives with someone less fortunate. But it wasn't Binky or Minda this was happening to! It was her!

Practice what you preach, Leighton! Where's your faith now?

Lexi clamped her hands over her ears but it didn't make the horrible voices in her head go away. Why was she feeling so selfish all of a sudden?

The sound of her mother's footsteps on the stairs made Lexi sit up and wipe away the tears that had squeezed onto her cheeks.

Mrs. Leighton knocked briefly and then came bursting into Lexi's room.

"Isn't she nice, Lexi? What a wonderful woman! I've never met anyone so caring or concerned about young people."

"Yeah. Nice."

"And she says that everything here looks good."

Lexi stared at her mother. She hadn't seen her look so happy or excited in a long time. What was the word for how her mother looked? A word her father or Mrs. Waverly might use . . . fulfilled. That was it. Her mother looked fulfilled, like she was finally doing the right thing and loving every minute of it.

"Anna says there is such a *desperate* need for homes right now that they might have a teenager for us by the end of the week!"

The end of the week? Lexi stifled a gasp. *So soon?*

"It will be good for all of us, Lexi, to share the wonderful life we have with someone less fortunate." Mrs. Leighton moved toward Lexi and gave her a gentle kiss on the forehead. "I feel so blessed to have you and Ben for my children."

Lexi watched as her mother left her room, closing the door behind her.

The end of the week.

It couldn't be. It just couldn't be. That was much too soon.

———

"All right, Lexi, what's with you?" Jennifer demanded the next afternoon at the Hamburger Shack. "You've been moping around for two days like you lost your best friend. 'Fess up. What's happened?"

Jennifer, Todd, Binky and Egg all stared at Lexi. They were sitting in a private booth near the back of the cafe. No one else was within hearing distance. Lexi studied the faces of her friends.

These were the people she cared most about in Cedar River. They'd lived through lots of things together in the past few months. If she couldn't tell them, who *could* she tell?

"My parents have applied to be foster parents."

"Huh?" Jennifer looked blank. "What's that?"

"What for?" was Binky's reaction. "Who wants more kids than they already have?"

Todd and Egg were silent.

Lexi answered Jennifer's question first. "My mom heard that there was a need for temporary housing for adolescents. Sometimes kids run away from home or can't live with their parents because of drug or alcohol problems or some other reason. Mom wants to provide a home for kids until they can go back into their own homes."

"So it's like . . . troublemakers . . . right?"

"Not always. Sometimes it's the parents who are having the troubles and they need time to sort out their lives."

Jennifer frowned. "I'd hate it. Who wants to share their house with a complete stranger? I mean really!"

"I agree," Binky said emphatically. "Who knows what kind of a person you might get? And all the time your mom usually spends with you she'll spend with the new kid!"

Egg wasn't quite so quick to condemn. "Maybe it would be all right . . . depending on the person. You might even make a new friend."

"Good try, Egg," Lexi groaned, "but even that doesn't make me feel any better."

"Why are your parents doing this, Lexi?" Todd wondered. He wasn't committing himself until he knew all the facts.

"My mother thinks God gave her gifts she should use to help other people—like mothering." Lexi sighed. "She *is* a great mom. I just don't know if I want to share her with somebody I don't even know!"

"Give it a try," Todd said. "Maybe you're worrying about something that isn't even going to be a problem. Give the situation a try before you make up your mind."

"Good old Todd," Jennifer snorted. "Always sensible. Still, I wouldn't like it."

Binky laid her hand across Lexi's. "I feel really bad for you, Lexi. I hope things work out."

"Yeah. If you need to get away, you can come to my house any time," Jennifer offered.

"Or ours," Egg chimed.

Even Todd nodded. "Call if it gets too bad. We can

take the car and go for a ride."

"Thanks, you guys." Lexi tried to smile, feeling like a mourner at a funeral. "I appreciate it."

Todd glanced at his watch. "Egg! We're supposed to meet Harry right now. We'd better get going."

Egg nodded and the two boys said their goodbyes. When they were gone, Jennifer leaned over the table and said to Lexi, "Frankly, I think this foster kid thing stinks. I don't like this person already and I haven't even met her!"

"Me too!" Binky chimed in. "I don't like her at all!"

"Thanks, guys, but Todd is right. We all have to give this thing a chance. I guess things were going too smoothly at our house. Maybe we need a shake-up."

"Who needs that?" Jennifer grumped. "Just remember, we're here if you need us."

Lexi considered her friends' conversation all the way to her father's office. Maybe they were all over-reacting. Maybe they wouldn't even get a foster kid. Maybe, if they did, Lexi would love this person!

And maybe the Emerald Tones' jackets will turn pink!

———

The office was quiet this afternoon. Lexi hummed as she fed the animals. The ferrets had gone home as had some of the dogs. A big black Persian cat with the name Prince Charles had come in, however. Prince Charles was as finicky as royalty, too. His owner had left little individual cans of cat food for him to eat. Apparently what Lexi's father served wasn't good enough.

Lexi petted Charles for a few moments before returning to the front office.

"I'm done with my chores," she announced to her dad's secretary. "I could sweep or answer phones, or—"

"Your dad is out on a call. He said to tell you that you didn't have to stay today since it will be very quiet. But thanks anyway."

"Sure." Lexi gathered her things and trudged toward home. It was a long walk, but she didn't mind. She had a lot of things to think through. It was still difficult for her to accept that someday soon there might be another teenager in her household.

———

There was no one downstairs when Lexi arrived at home. She could hear music blaring from the radio in her bedroom. Curious, she took the stairs two at a time to find out what was going on.

Ben and Mrs. Leighton were in the hallway. The door to Lexi's room was open as was that of the spare bedroom.

"Hi, Lexi! Home so soon?"

"Dad went on house calls."

"Oh. Good. Then you can help us."

"What are you doing?"

"I'm fixing up the spare bedroom. Anna assured me that we'd be getting a foster girl sooner or later and I wanted to be ready. What do you think?"

Lexi poked her head into the spare bedroom. It looked all fresh and pretty, as though her mother had just finished some heavy-duty spring housecleaning. There was a new bedspread and pillow sham on the bed and a fresh flower in a bud vase on the table by the window.

Then Lexi's eyes grew wide. "Isn't that my radio? And my stuffed animals?"

Mrs. Leighton nodded. "I thought it would be nice to make the room seem more homey. I hope you don't mind. You always use your other radio and, well, you have so many stuffed animals I thought you'd never notice that these were gone."

"Pretty flower!" Ben announced as he walked through the room to touch the daisy in the vase.

"We don't have flowers in our rooms," Lexi pointed out softly, knowing already that her mother wasn't going to realize the impact of her statement.

"I know that, Lexi. But we want our guest to feel at home here, don't we? We have to do everything we can to make that possible."

It was understandable, Lexi supposed, as she gazed about the sunny, inviting room, but Lexi herself was beginning to feel less and less at home here all the time.

Chapter Seven

"Want to go to the Hamburger Shack after school?" Todd asked as he and Lexi put the final touches on the most recent photographs for the *River Review*.

Lexi touched the corner of one of the photographs she had taken of the Cedar River track team and shook her head slowly. "No, I'd better not. I have to go to my dad's office and do some work for him tonight."

Todd nodded. "That's keeping you pretty busy, isn't it?"

Lexi shrugged. "I suppose so. It's nice to get a check every week, too."

Todd grinned. "That can't hurt. I'm thinking about repainting my car. I suppose I should put a few extra hours in at Mike's garage to earn enough to cover the cost." He looked at the big Seth Thomas clock on the wall and closed the file he was working on. "In fact, since you aren't free tonight, maybe that's what I'll do after school."

"Just because I can't go? Don't let that ruin your fun."

"Everything's just a little more fun when you're there, Lexi."

Then Todd's expression turned serious. "Except you have been rather . . . preoccupied lately."

Lexi nodded and tugged at a wisp of her hair. "I know, I'm sorry. It's this foster parent program that my mom and dad have gotten themselves into."

"Worrying about it isn't going to make it any better," Todd pointed out logically.

Lexi flung herself into a hard-backed folding chair. "I know it, but I can't seem to stop. I know it's my responsibility to honor whatever their wishes are, but, I have this really bad feeling about some stranger moving into our house."

Todd frowned. "You make it sound like it's going to be permanent. I thought you said these kids only stayed a few days."

"Sometimes a few days," Lexi agreed, "and sometimes a few weeks, or a few months. . . ."

Todd whistled low. "Well, you'll just have to hope it's one that only comes for a few days. Or, maybe you'll like her and want her to stay."

"Maybe," Lexi said doubtfully. "But, I don't think so."

"Give it a chance. Who knows?"

Who knows? The question echoed dully in Lexi's mind as she took the bus to her father's veterinary clinic. Maybe all this fretting and worrying was for nothing. She hoped so. She hoped this tied-up feeling she had in her stomach was created by her own imagination and not by some instinct that what her par-

ents were getting themselves into was going to be all
wrong.

Her mother was certainly looking forward to having their first placement come. She'd been baking
every day, cookies, cakes and casseroles for the
freezer so she wouldn't have to spend much time in
the kitchen the first days after the placement came.
Lexi was feeling slighted. She couldn't remember her
mother attacking meals for them with such enthusiasm.

The veterinary clinic was very busy. There were
seven or eight cars parked in the front parking lot.
When Lexi went inside, she saw that her father's
secretary looked extremely harried. There was a big,
black lab straining at his leash and looking hungrily
at a basket of tiny kittens on the far side of the room.
Occasionally, the lab would let out a loud woofing
noise that made everyone jump and look askance at
the drooling animal.

"Lexi! I'm so glad you've come," Mrs. Harmon
gasped. "Would you run to the post office for me and
mail these letters and pick up another roll of stamps?
And when you come back, feed the animals in the
cages. They're getting very noisy. I wonder if a little
food wouldn't make them less restless."

Lexi smiled and nodded. At least here she felt
useful and needed. Most days she wondered how her
father and his staff had gotten along without her.

Lexi noted when she went back to feed the animals that the pets in the back room had changed
again since she'd last been there. Her father normally requested that the pets needing surgery be
brought in the night before and kept at least twenty-

four hours. Most times, eager pet owners were there to pick up their animals by the end of the next day.

She'd just finished filling the water dishes when her father's secretary poked her head through the door. "Lexi? Would you mind answering the phones for me for a few minutes? I've needed to run some errands all day and it's been so busy that I haven't even had time to take a breath until just now."

"Sure." Lexi liked working at the reception desk. That was far more interesting than changing litter boxes and hosing out cages. She hadn't been working there ten minutes when a familiar voice responded to her greeting of "Leighton Veterinary Clinic. How may I help you?"

"Lexi? Is that you?"

"Mom?"

"Yes, dear. You're manning the telephone today, I hear."

"Just for a few minutes while Dad's secretary runs some errands."

"Good for you, honey. I'm glad to see he's keeping you busy." Mrs. Leighton's voice had a bright, happy lilt that reminded Lexi of the chiming of faraway bells.

"Mom? Did something happen?" Lexi wondered.

There was a quick pause on the other end of the line. "Happen? No, everything's fine, Lexi, just fine. In fact, I'm just on my way out to get Ben. He was invited to play at a friend's house after school tonight. Someone he met at the Academy. Isn't that nice? I'm supposed to pick him up at five. May I speak to your father for a moment, Lexi?"

"Sure, I'll buzz him." A few minutes later Lexi

stared long and hard at the little red light on the telephone indicating that her mother and father were still on the line. Something had happened. Lexi knew it. She could feel it. She could hear it in her mother's voice, but her mother was not willing to tell her what it was. That made Lexi uncomfortable. She and her mother had never kept secrets from each other before.

It was nearly six o'clock by the time her father had finished the last of his duties. He came out into the reception area. "Are you ready to go, Lexi? Looks like we're going to be late for supper if we don't hurry."

Lexi nodded and gathered up the school books she had been studying while she waited for her father. "Anytime. Once it quieted down here, I thought I'd do some studying."

Mr. Leighton nodded. "That's fine with me. I'm just glad to have you here to help out when we need you."

"It's been fairly busy," Lexi said with a smile. "I haven't felt useless."

Mr. Leighton chuckled. "You'll never be useless in our lives, Lexi. Remember that."

Her father was more quiet than usual on the drive toward home, Lexi noted. It was as though he had something on his mind. Then, about four blocks away from the Leighton household, he turned to glance at Lexi.

"Honey? Your mom called this afternoon."

"I know. I answered the phone."

"She had some news."

"Oh?" A nervous sensation spiraled in Lexi's midsection.

"She called to say that Social Services was bringing over a foster girl."

"Already? Tonight?" Lexi felt a hard knot in her stomach. She wasn't ready for this. Not tonight. She needed more time.

"Your mother expected them to be at the house when she returned with Ben."

"Don't they have to do something with her first? Process her or fill out forms or anything?"

Lexi realized that she was pressing down hard with her foot against the floor boards, as if to try and stop the car from the course it was taking nearer and nearer their home.

"Don't look so glum, Lexi. I think this is going to be a good experience for all of us," her father attempted to reassure her. All he managed to do was make her feel even more lost and nervous.

Too quickly they arrived at home. Lexi took her time gathering her books together and dragging her feet toward the front door. Somehow she found it difficult to put one foot in front of the other. *My shoes must have turned to lead,* she thought wryly.

"Here they are! Finally!" Mrs. Leighton came to the door. Her voice sounded a little too bright and her expression seemed a little too fixed. "Come in. Come in, Lexi. Come in, Jim. I want you to meet Amanda."

Lexi followed her mother into the living room where a petite girl with blond hair and large brown eyes perched on the edge of the couch. She was attractive, Lexi thought immediately, in a dramatic sort of way. Her face was heart-shaped and the dark chocolate colored eyes dominated her face. Amanda had a shapely nose and mobile lips which Lexi sensed could either turn into a wide smile or a very sullen pout at will. At the moment, the girl's dark eyes were darting from side to side taking in the strange living room and the nervous family hovering near the mother.

"Amanda? This is my daughter, Alexis—we call her Lexi—and my husband, Dr. James Leighton."

Amanda glanced upward and out of the corners of her eyes at Lexi's father. "Dr. Leighton?" she echoed. The label seemed to impress her.

"He's a veterinarian."

"Oh. Not a real doctor?"

"A veterinarian is a real doctor," Lexi protested. "For animals."

"Not a people doctor," Amanda corrected.

"No, you're right about that," Mr. Leighton chuckled and put out a hand in greeting. "Definitely not a people doctor."

Lexi looked at her father's stance. Why didn't he seem insulted by Amanda's implication that a veterinarian was not as important or significant as a doctor for humans? She was downright insulting and her father hadn't even seemed to notice!

"Lexi goes to Cedar River High School," Mrs. Leighton said brightly. "That's where you'll be going, too, Amanda."

Amanda looked at Lexi again with the same sort of interest that one might study a bug under a microscope. "Oh," she said flatly.

"I've called the school about getting you enrolled in classes."

Amanda shrugged. "I don't care. I don't like school anyway."

Mrs. Leighton laughed nervously, obviously not quite at ease with this solemn looking girl who had landed on her couch. "Well, that doesn't mean we can let you skip it."

Amanda looked at her sharply and Lexi had a certain hunch that part of Amanda's problems had involved truancy at school.

Lexi turned beseeching eyes to her mother. *Oh, Mom, why did you get us into this,* she thought.

"Supper's almost ready," Mrs. Leighton said as she glanced at her watch. "In fact, I think I'll just go into the kitchen for a moment and put things on the table. Lexi, why don't you visit with Amanda while I—"

Amanda's eyes darted immediately to Mrs. Leighton. The girl might be sullen and unfriendly, but it was obvious that she had already bonded to Lexi's mother and did not want to be left alone with Jim and Lexi.

Just then, Ben ambled into the living room, dragging a toy shovel and singing a song slightly off key.

"Benjamin," Mrs. Leighton said. "I'd like you to meet Amanda."

Ben stared at the girl on the couch for a long moment before echoing, " 'Manda."

"Amanda," the girl corrected him, looking doubtfully at the small boy. "What's wrong with him?" she asked bluntly.

Mrs. Leighton looked slightly taken aback. "Ben has Down's syndrome, Amanda, but it's not polite to simply blurt out a question like—"

"Oh, retarded," the girl deduced. She gave Ben one last glance as if to dismiss him and turned away slightly.

So that's what "giving someone the cold shoulder" was, Lexi thought to herself. She'd never quite known what that meant before, but Amanda's shoulder had turned away from Ben and it had certainly been cold.

Ben looked a little puzzled by the response he had received, then shrugged and continued on his way through the living room, still singing slightly off-key.

Mr. Leighton tried to fill the awkward silence in the room by ushering everyone to the dinner table. Lexi moved to sit in her usual place, but her mother stepped out of the kitchen to say "No, no, Lexi, why don't you sit over here and let Amanda sit there?"

Lexi looked up, startled, "But that's my—"

"I know you don't mind sitting over here by me, Lexi," her mother said with a bite of steel in her tone. "Please."

Resignedly, Lexi took the chair opposite Amanda. First it was her radio and her stuffed animal. Now it was her chair at the dinner table. How many things was she going to have to give up for this sullen stranger?

———

"More potatoes, Amanda?" Mrs. Leighton asked. "My goodness, you've hardly eaten a thing."

Amanda shook her head disinterestedly, "Don't like potatoes."

"Broccoli, then, with cheese sauce."

Amanda shook her head again. "Don't like broccoli."

"More meat?"

Amanda dropped her eyes and gazed at the table top. "Full."

Lexi ground her molars together in frustration. If she'd been the one to announce at the table that she didn't like vegetables of any kind, or meat that wasn't fried in butter, or anything with onions in it, Mrs. Leighton would have scolded her soundly and told her to change her ways. Since it was Amanda, Lexi's mother nodded her head worriedly, almost apologetic for the delicious meal she'd cooked.

Mrs. Leighton took the napkin off her lap and laid it next to her plate. "Well, Lexi, one thing I suppose we should discuss is arrangements for going to school tomorrow."

Lexi looked up in surprise. "Arrangements? I'll just go at my normal time and—"

"I think you'd better go early tomorrow, dear, so you have some extra time to show Amanda the ropes."

Lexi glanced at Amanda who was glaring at her. The last thing she felt like doing right now was show-ing this girl anything. So far, she had managed to insult Mrs. Leighton's cooking, Ben's handicap and Mr. Leighton's profession. Lexi shuddered to think what Amanda was thinking about her.

"Ben will show Amanda his toys," Ben an-nounced brightly in an attempt to join the conver-sation. "Toys, toys, toys."

Amanda glanced at the little boy sharply and then looked away as if what she saw disgusted her.

"That's very nice of you, Ben. Isn't it Amanda?" Mrs. Leighton asked.

"Yeah, nice," Amanda muttered, but she didn't look Ben's way.

Lexi curled her fingers into fists in her lap. Poor Ben was only trying to be helpful. Helpful and vying for a little of the attention that his mother seemed determined to shower on this unpleasant girl.

"I'd like to see your toys," Lexi said defiantly, "Have you gotten some new ones, Ben?" knowing very well he hadn't.

Ben nodded cheerfully. "New toys, old toys, toys."

"Well, why don't you show me your toys before you go to bed tonight? I'll come in and tell you a bedtime story."

The expression on Ben's face brightened and a shimmer of hurt bled through Lexi. Couldn't her parents see what this awful girl had done to Ben?

Mrs. Leighton pushed her chair away from the table. When she stood up, she was winding her fingers together nervously. "Lexi, why don't you take Amanda upstairs and show her your room and the room she's going to be sleeping in?"

Lexi bit back the response that she had many better things to do and stood up. "Come on, Amanda."

They mounted the stairs together. From the corner of her eye, Lexi could see Amanda staring to the right and to the left without comment. The first room they came to was Lexi's. Lexi opened the door and allowed Amanda to step in ahead of her. "This is my bedroom," Lexi explained.

Without hesitation, Amanda moved into the room and started walking around its perimeter. She ran a finger across the chest of drawers, touching this item and that without compulsion. Her eyes scanned the walls.

"Kind of babyish for someone your age, isn't it?" she asked bluntly.

Lexi was startled. "No, I don't think so."

"Ruffles and stuffed animals and even a sewing machine," Amanda sneered. "Who lives here anyway? Susie Homemaker?"

Lexi tossed the dust cover over her sewing machine. "I like to sew."

Amanda's gaze flitted across the outfit Lexi wore. "Yeah, well, I always thought it was really easy to tell homemade clothes from store bought."

"It can be, if it's not a good seamstress doing the sewing."

"And you're a good seamstress?" Amanda asked with a sneer.

Lexi's chin came up in the air. "I like to think I am."

"I was right the first time," Amanda said mockingly. "This is Susie Homemaker's room. Where's mine?"

Silently, Lexi led the way down the hall to the guest room that Mrs. Leighton had prepared for Amanda. She flung open the door and led the way into the bedroom. With a start, Lexi noticed that her favorite poster, which had been hanging on the back of her closet door for months, had been transferred into the guest room and was now looking down over Amanda's bed. *The least Mother could have done is ask before she took that poster,* Lexi thought to herself irately.

Lexi glanced at Amanda who was staring from the poster to Lexi and back again. A small humorless smile twisted at Amanda's lip. With a sinking sensation, Lexi realized that Amanda knew that the poster had come into her bedroom without Lexi's permission.

"Nice poster," Amanda commented. "Now, that one, I like. The last house I was in had lots of posters in my bedroom."

Lexi bit back the questions she wanted to ask. Who was Amanda anyway? Where did she come from? Why couldn't she live in her own home? Had she been a runaway? There were so many things that Lexi wanted to know!

Amanda flung herself down on the bed and picked up one of the stuffed animals that was propped against the pillow. "Yours?" she asked Lexi.

Lexi nodded. "Mom thought they might make your room feel a little more cozy."

Amanda's eyes went to the radio and then to the poster. Then she nodded smugly.

Lexi again experienced that dreadful, sinking sensation in the pit of her stomach. This girl had already read the situation in the Leighton household. She already knew that Lexi's mother was going to be her strongest ally. Lexi had no doubt that Amanda would be willing to use that knowledge against her anytime it was necessary.

There was going to be trouble. Lexi could see it. She could feel it. She could practically taste it. She didn't know yet what kind of trouble it would be, but deep in her heart, she knew that Amanda was trouble and she was going to cause more of it for Lexi.

"Are you girls having fun getting acquainted?" Mrs. Leighton asked from the doorway. She was still wiping her hands dry on the corner of a dish towel.

"Right. Fun," Amanda said. Only Lexi noticed the sarcasm in her voice.

"Very good. By the way, I rented a movie for us

to watch this evening. Shall we all go downstairs? It's supposed to be a wonderful comedy. I thought it might be a good way for Amanda to relax on her first night here."

Lexi's eyebrow arched in surprise. Her mother never rented tapes for them to watch. She always called it a waste of time. *Of course,* Lexi mused, *that was before Amanda.*

"Thanks, Mom, but I have a lot of homework," Lexi sighed. "And I promised to look at Ben's toys."

"Oh, well, you'd better get that done first," Mrs. Leighton nodded. "Afterwards, why don't you come downstairs and join us?" She reached out an arm and slipped it around Amanda's shoulders. "Amanda and I will just go down and turn the tape on. You join us as soon as you can."

Lexi nodded numbly and watched her mother and Amanda descend to the first floor.

It was after ten when Lexi finished her work. The movie was over and her mother and father were in the kitchen eating ice cream sundaes with Amanda. Ben had long ago fallen asleep and been carried to bed.

Rather than interrupt the intimate little scene, Lexi washed her face and brushed her teeth and went quietly back to her bedroom. She lay on the bed staring at the ceiling for a long while. Eventually, she heard Amanda and her parents mount the stairs and say their good-nights. Even after the house was silent, sleep didn't come.

Finally, desperately, Lexi slid out of her bed, and knelt down with her forehead on the rounded corner of her mattress and her eyes squeezed tightly shut.

"Oh help, God," she prayed. "What am I going to do? I don't like her, Lord, and I know she doesn't like me. How am I ever going to make this work?" Lexi prayed, but the cold hard lumps that had been in her heart remained unthawed. Finally, sadly, she crawled back into bed.

Even praying didn't seem to help tonight, Lexi thought bitterly. Where was God tonight? Had He moved away from her? Or, she thought sadly, was it she that had moved away from Him?

Chapter Eight

"I've got everything straightened out in the administration's office," Mrs. Leighton announced to Amanda and Lexi as the girls stood outside the glass walled room. "They even gave me your schedule, Amanda, and sketched out a map. Lexi can show you where your rooms are, can't you Lexi?"

Lexi nodded, squelching the idea that she'd like to show Amanda to all the *wrong* rooms for her classes. She gave herself a mental scolding. It had been a bad morning, that's all.

"Lexi can show you where your rooms are, can't you Lexi?"

"Lexi will let you use one of her blouses today, won't you Lexi?"

"Lexi will go into the shower later."

"Lexi will eat that toast if you don't want it."

"Lexi will . . ."

By eight-thirty in the morning Lexi was already feeling like a doormat beneath Amanda's feet. Granted, her mother was trying to be nice, but it seemed to Lexi that she didn't have to be nice at her own daughter's expense!

Lexi sighed. "Come on, Amanda, I'll show you where your locker is. Number 125, right?"

When Lexi glanced back, she could see her mother still standing by the administrator's door, looking hopeful and a little forlorn. Lexi sighed. Her mother wanted this to work out so badly! The least she could do was be nice to Amanda. After all, she didn't even know Amanda's history yet. Maybe there was something horrible in her background that justified her acting sullen and nasty.

"Here it is. One-twenty-five. And your first class is right across the hall. Your next class is—"

"I'll find it."

"Okay, but if you need help—"

"I don't need help from you or from anyone."

Lexi bit her lip. "Sorry."

Amanda flung her jacket into the locker and pushed the door shut. "Where's the pop machine?"

"They don't allow food in class, but—"

"I don't care. Where is it?"

It took all of Lexi's will power to keep from pointing out that Amanda had drunk all the orange juice this morning and not even left a glass for her or Ben. Why did she want pop now?

"Down to the corner and hang a right." *Let her drown from the inside out—see if I care.*

"Okay."

Amanda was about to take off when a young man's voice yelled, "Hey, Lexi!" She paused and stared curiously at the threesome coming down the hallway.

"Hi, Egg, Binky, Jennifer."

"Hi, yourself. Who's your friend?" Egg stared curiously at Amanda. "This is Amanda Remer. She's—you know—staying with us for a while."

Immediately, all three of her friends began to nod. Binky stared at Amanda with interest.

"Welcome to Cedar River," Egg began. He thrust out his hand for a welcoming shake, but Amanda averted her eyes and he dropped his arm limply.

Binky shot Amanda a daggered look. *Binky* could run down Egg all she wanted, but when anyone else was rude to him, *look out!*

Jennifer, who was always more cool and collected than Binky, gave Amanda a once-over stare as if to size her up. Amanda returned the steady gaze for a moment before turning away as if distinterested. Jennifer's eyebrow notched upward. "Nice to meet you, too," she said sarcastically under her breath.

Lexi laid a hand on Jennifer's arm. "See you at noon?"

Jennifer glanced at Amanda. "I suppose. Does she—"

Lexi pinched Jennifer and mouthed "Be quiet!"

Jennifer shrugged, uncaring. Already there was an obvious tension between her and Amanda.

The first warning bell rang. Egg, Binky and Jennifer scattered quickly, leaving Amanda and Lexi alone.

"Brother! What a bunch of jerks!" Amanda sneered. "Did you see the Adam's apple on that guy? And that ugly little person with him? Yuk. Where does she shop? Garage sales?"

"They're my friends!" Lexi protested furiously. "You have no right to say horrible things about them!"

Amanda shrugged. "Says who? If you want to hang around with two Munchkins and the Wicked Witch of the North, I can't stop you, but I'd watch out for that blond. She's the kind that could turn on you."

Lexi's mouth nearly gaped open. How could she talk about Jennifer like that? Jennifer was one of her most loyal, true-blue friends! Still, and Lexi eyed Amanda, maybe Amanda didn't like Jennifer because she could stand up to her. Amanda could roll over Binky and Egg like a steamroller over tin cans, but Jennifer . . . she was a different story. Lexi filed that bit of information away in her head. If she ever needed help with Amanda, maybe Jennifer was the one who could do it.

"You're going to be late."

Lexi spun around to see Todd grinning down at her. His dark blue eyes were twinkling and his golden hair was just crying out for someone to touch it.

"Who's this?" He stared at Amanda briefly, then turned his smile toward her.

Suddenly, a transformation took place before Lexi's very eyes. The sullen, pouty look about Amanda's mouth softened. She licked her lower lip and smiled. Her eyes, which had been narrowed and darting about, focused intently on Todd's smile. Her eyelashes fluttered, her demeanor shifted from pouty to kittenish.

"My name is Amanda Remer." She batted her

eyelashes. "And who are *you?*"

"Amanda, this is Todd Winston," Lexi blurted, suddenly feeling very left out. Todd seemed immobilized by Amanda's smile. "Todd, Amanda is staying with us." She put as much emphasis as she could on "staying with us," trying to hint that this was the intruder that had come to roost at her front door.

"Nice to meet you, Amanda. Welcome to Cedar River."

"I'm glad to be here," Amanda cooed. "Especially now."

Lexi was going to gag. She might even throw up right here, all over Todd and Amanda's shoes.

Thankfully, Todd glanced at his watch and muttered, "Oh, oh. I've got to go. I need to stop at my locker before class." With a quick wave, he turned and jogged off down the hall.

Amanda was staring dreamily after him when Lexi turned to her.

"What a hunk! He's adorable."

And mine! Lexi wanted to scream. Instead she murmured, "Todd and I are very good friends." The emphasis was on *very*.

Amanda eyed Lexi knowingly. "Oh, so that's how it is." She shrugged. "Well, he's cute. I'm glad to see there are some neat guys in this school. That's promising."

Lexi didn't pursue the conversation any further. It was time for class. Besides, she had this horrible thought rattling around in her mind that made it impossible for her to speak.

She and Amanda separated but the idea still haunted her.

Terrific. Not only am I losing my own mother to this Amanda person, now she's going to want Todd, too!

With an empty feeling in her stomach, Lexi went to class.

———

Amanda, it seemed, was a chameleon. Just like the little lizards Lexi's father kept in a large glass terrarium in the office waiting room, she could change moods and colors to fit whatever surrounding she was in. She could be sweet and charming one moment and nasty the next. Lexi deduced that she was the only one "fortunate" enough to see both sides of Amanda's personality.

Amanda had a sharp, unerring instinct for picking out the people who were popular, influential and interesting. The rest appeared to be second-class citizens in her mind, hardly worthy of her attention. Todd, Chad Allen and Matt Windsor were in the first group. Binky and Egg were in the second.

Lexi and Amanda were standing in the hallway studying Amanda's class schedule. The noon bell had just rung and the hallways were filling with students. From the corner of her eye, Lexi noticed Minda coming their way.

"Hi, Lexi," Minda babbled. "Isn't it just frantic in here today?" As she talked, she eyed Amanda up and down. "Who is this? A new friend?"

Lexi drew a deep breath. "Minda, this is Amanda Remer. She's going to be staying with us for . . . a while." Lexi grimanced. She didn't even know how long this person would be staying with her family!

Any length of time was too long.

"So you're the new kid living with Lexi." Minda nodded thoughtfully, obviously processing all the information she'd gathered from rumors around the school.

Lexi took a step back and watched Minda and Amanda interact. *Here were two of a kind,* Lexi thought to herself. It might be interesting to see which of these two would come out on top in a battle of words.

Knowing Minda as well as she did, Lexi could tell that she wasn't terribly impressed with Amanda. Still, there was a flicker of genuine interest in Minda's eyes. After all, Minda might find Amanda . . . useful.

"So how do you like it so far?" Minda asked, testing the waters.

Amanda flipped her wavy blond hair and lifted one shoulder. "Kind of boring so far. I hope it gets better."

Minda looked amused. "Oh? Boring? At Leighton's?"

Amanda's lip curled. "You said it. I didn't."

Minda started to smile. "Of course, Lexi's never been known for her wild parties or anything like that."

"I can imagine."

They were talking about her as if she weren't even there and Lexi didn't even care. She could see what was going on. Amanda had found someone who was in Category Number One—popular, influential, interesting—and she was pursuing it full steam ahead.

Minda, on the other hand, had just met someone who could irritate Lexi in ways she couldn't, living in the Leighton household as she was. Lexi could see Minda softening.

"So," Minda began. "Have you eaten lunch yet?"

Amanda's eyes brightened. "No."

"Want to join us? The Hi-Fives, I mean. It's this social club we have that's really radical."

Amanda didn't even look twice at Lexi. Instead, she fell into step with Minda. "So tell me about these Hi-Fives. I mean, like, how do you get into the club. I mean, are they all as great-looking as you. You could be a model or something, do you know that. . . ."

Lexi sighed and slumped backward against a locker. "Goodbye and good riddance!" she muttered under her breath. At least she could eat her lunch in peace.

"How's it going?" Jennifer was peering into Lexi's face when she opened her eyes.

"Running its course—like the bubonic plague."

"She's a brat, isn't she?"

"The worst."

"Where is she now?"

"Having lunch with Minda and the Hi-Fives."

Jennifer whistled. "That didn't take long."

"It was inevitable, I suppose. She managed to win Minda over with a few snide remarks about me."

Jennifer shrugged. "You know Minda. She likes to have 'dirt' on everyone. What better way to get it on you than through someone living in your own house?"

"Someone who doesn't like me!"

"Are you sure about that?"

"Positive. The girl is a witch! Besides, Amanda was already fawning up to Minda so that I wanted to gag. 'You could be a model or something. . . .' "

"Yuk!"

"I know it. You know how Minda loves that kind of thing."

"She's in for sure, then? With Minda's crowd, I mean?"

"Unless she blows it." Lexi shrugged. "Maybe I don't care. Maybe I should be relieved. If Amanda spends her time with Minda, then she won't have to spend it with me."

She closed her eyes for a moment, and when she opened them, there was pain and frustration in their expression. "What's wrong with me, Jennifer? Listen to me? Do I sound like a Christian is supposed to sound? What's happening to me?"

"Amanda Remer is what's happening to you," Jennifer said frankly.

Lexi nodded morosely. "Maybe she's a test."

"A test?"

"Yeah. A trial," Lexi said gloomily. "Something to see how strong my faith is. Something to make me strong and a better Christian if I live through the experience."

Jennifer gave Lexi a compassionate look. "If there's anything I can do. . . ."

Lexi shook her head. "I have no business acting the way I am. Amanda has problems. If she didn't, she wouldn't need to be in a foster home. As soon as I get the opportunity, I'm going to find out more about her. She arrived so unexpectedly that Mom and

Dad and I didn't have time to talk. What I need to do is be more understanding, that's all."

Understanding. That was the key, Lexi told herself. *Compassion. Forgiveness.*

Those are the attitudes that would get her through this time with Amanda the Chameleon. Lexi chewed thoughtfully on her lower lip. Amanda was going to be like living with an entire *group* of girls—the harsh, critical girl who disliked Egg and Binky, the sickenly sweet person who tried to charm Todd and Minda, and the real Amanda, who didn't try to hide any of her emotions from Lexi.

"Oh, help, God!" Lexi pleaded. "I'm really going to need it!"

Chapter Nine

"More beef stroganoff, Amanda? Another spoonful of fruit salad, perhaps?" Mrs. Leighton hovered over the dining room table like a hummingbird over the bird feeder in the back yard. "I'm delighted to see what a good appetite you have. Wasn't it lucky that I made your favorite meal?"

Lexi rolled her eyes and slid a little lower in her chair. Ben played listlessly with a noodle on his plate. They were both getting tired of the way Mrs. Leighton fluttered about Amanda. Stroganoff was one of *their* favorite meals, too, and Mrs. Leighton didn't seem particularly delighted about that.

"There are cream puffs for dessert. Lexi, do you want to bring them from the kitchen?"

"I'm too full for a cream puff right now," Amanda announced.

Mrs. Leighton frowned. "Oh, well then, maybe we could all have some later, just before bedtime. That might be nice."

"Ben wants a cream puff," Ben announced emphatically. "Now!"

"Oh, Ben, you can wait a little bit."

Ben's lower lip jutted out in an unaccustomed pout.

"Well, then, I'll just do up the dishes and we'll have our dessert a little bit later."

Lexi stood up. "I can help you, Mom." She glanced sideways at Amanda.

Amanda's gaze seemed fixed on an invisible spot on the floor.

The least you could do is offer to help, Lexi thought to herself. She could see that her mother was unsure whether to include Amanda in their nightly ritual of cleaning up the kitchen after dinner or not. Lexi had overheard Anna McNeil tell her mother that they would be offering some classes for new foster parents. Lexi grimaced. She was beginning to wonder if her mother didn't need one right away. Amanda already seemed to have the upper hand in the household.

Without comment, Lexi carried dishes to the kitchen, rinsed them and put them in the dishwasher. By the time she'd finished, her parents were sitting in the living room visiting with Amanda.

"Come and join us, Lexi," Mrs. Leighton invited. "Amanda is just telling us about the last school that she went to and how it compares to Cedar River."

Lexi glanced out at the driveway. "I'd love to, but I'm expecting Binky and Jennifer to come over. We were going to listen to some new tapes."

Amanda straightened a little at her perch on the couch. She looked very self-righteous as she announced, "Well, *I* planned to study this evening."

Mrs. Leighton smiled at her. "Good for you,

Amanda. That's the kind of attitude I like to hear. Don't you agree, Lexi?"

What am I supposed to say? Lexi wondered to herself. *That studying was a wonderful idea and her own plan to listen to tapes sounded pretty shoddy and irresponsible in comparison?* Everything seemed to be a no-win situation today. Lexi was glad to hear the doorbell ring. Jennifer and Binky were standing outside, each holding an armful of tapes.

"Are we late?" Jennifer wondered.

"Just in time," Lexi muttered under her breath. "Just in time to save me."

"Save you?" Binky echoed. "What do you mean. . . ?" Her gaze fell on Amanda looking down from the top of the stairs to where they stood. "Oh, never mind. I get it now."

After saying hello to Mr. and Mrs. Leighton, the two girls followed Lexi upstairs to her room. Amanda had disappeared and the door to the guest room was closed solidly.

"I just got a new tape that you're really going to like," Lexi announced as she flipped open the lid on her cassette holder. "I bought it at the mall last Saturday. Wait 'til you hear it." Then she stared into the tape case. "Where is it?"

"You haven't even looked, Lexi. How can you tell it's missing?"

"Because over half of my tapes are missing," Lexi yelped. "Look."

Jennifer and Binky peered into the case. "Did you move them? Maybe you put them into a drawer," Binky suggested as she eyed the dresser.

Lexi shook her head emphatically. "I haven't

touched those tapes." Then her eyes narrowed. "But I do have a sneaking suspicion where they are."

With a firm foot step and arms swinging, Lexi strode to her bedroom door and flung it open. She was halfway down the hall before Binky and Jennifer caught up to her. She raised her arm and knocked loudly on Amanda's door.

"Yes?" said Amanda in a syrupy, sweet voice. "What is it?"

"Open the door, Amanda, it's Lexi."

"Oh," the voice suddenly turned cool. "I'm studying. I need to be alone."

"Open the door, Amanda. I want my tapes."

"Tapes? I don't know what you're talking about. Go away."

"The tapes that were in my bedroom and are now in yours. Open the door and let me get them."

"How do you know I have the tapes?" Amanda said, her voice muffled by the door.

"Because I have no doubt that my mother put them in there. I would like to use them. Now open the door, please."

"If your mother put them in here for me to use, why don't you let me use them," Amanda said. There was a note of belligerence in her voice. "I'll look around and give them back to you tomorrow."

"Jennifer and Binky are here now, Amanda." Lexi was becoming even more irritated.

"What's going on up here, girls?" Mrs. Leighton wondered as she mounted the stairs. "Did I hear loud voices?"

"Amanda won't let me into her room to get my tapes," Lexi said shortly.

"Oh, I'm sure that's not true," Mrs. Leighton said lightly. "I suppose I should have asked you before I moved some of your tapes into the other bedroom. I thought she'd enjoy having some music for her room as well."

"Fine," Lexi muttered, "but I want to use them right now. Make her open her door."

Just then, the bedroom door glided open and Amanda stood framed in the doorway. "Yes, Lexi? Did you want something?" She said sweetly.

"I want my tapes."

"Oh, of course. Come on in and get them. I haven't had a chance to listen to any of them yet, but I'm sure they're wonderful."

Mrs. Leighton gave Lexi a puzzled glance as if wondering why Lexi had thought she needed to use such a loud, harsh voice to get Amanda to open the door. "See Lexi? That was easy," Mrs. Leighton said with a hint of reproach in her voice. "All you had to do was knock."

"I did knock, several times," Lexi pointed out stubbornly. "She wouldn't let me in."

"Well, you had to knock so I could hear you," Amanda pointed out indignantly.

"You did hear me." It took all of Lexi's will power not to shout. "You did hear me. You just didn't want to let me in because my friends are here and we wanted to listen to tapes."

"Lexi," Mrs. Leighton warned.

Sudden tears sprang to Amanda's eyes. "You're just being mean and cruel, Lexi Leighton, and you're saying those things to make me feel bad."

Lexi was as stunned as everyone else by Amanda's intense response.

Mrs. Leighton took the last three steps to the top of the stairs in great haste. "That's enough girls, right now. Stop it, both of you."

Jennifer and Binky stared at the threesome with large, round eyes and gaping mouths. Mrs. Leighton turned to the pair apologetically. "Jennifer, Binky, I'm afraid that you girls are going to have to go home now. It seems we have some things to settle here tonight and I believe it would be best to do it without extra visitors."

Binky's head was bobbing up and down like one of those little doggie car ornaments that sometimes rode in backs of windows. She stepped backward toward Lexi's bedroom. "We'll just get our stuff—"

"—and get out of here," Jennifer finished for her.

"I do think that's best tonight." Mrs. Leighton looked very sad and very tired. "I think this has been a hard day for all of us."

Jennifer and Binky grabbed their things and hurried back into the hallway and down the stairs. Lexi was still standing, staring angrily at Amanda when she heard the front door slam.

"Now then, girls, exactly what is going on here?"

"She wouldn't let me in the room to get my tapes," Lexi said dully.

Amanda wore an innocent expression. "I didn't even hear her knock, Mrs. Leighton. She just got so angry so quickly."

"Lexi, was that necessary?"

Lexi turned toward her mother, fury sparking in her eyes. "She's lying, Mother. She heard me. She knew what I wanted."

"That's not so, Lexi. You're just saying that to

make me look bad," Amanda protested. Her large dark eyes looked hurt and innocent.

"If I can't get a straight story from either of you girls, then I think you both better just spend the rest of the evening confined to your bedrooms. You both have studying to do, and at the same time, you can think about the ways in which you treat others."

Lexi's mouth gaped like that of a fish. She hadn't been sent to her room as punishment since she was a tiny girl. A rush of humiliation sped through her and she spun around. As she did so, she caught the look of triumph on Amanda's face.

Amanda doesn't care if she's confined to her room, Lexi thought furiously. That's where she was planning to spend the evening anyway. She just didn't want me to have Jennifer and Binky over and be having fun without her.

That realization didn't make Lexi feel any better, especially when she heard the sound of the TV and Ben's laughter downstairs in the living room.

———

"Lexi?" Mrs. Leighton's voice was soft, nearly a whisper and the knock on Lexi's door barely more than feathers brushing across the wood.

"Come in," Lexi mumbled. She'd gone to bed early since there was nothing else to do. She'd read awhile and turned out her light, but for the last half hour, Lexi had been lying in the darkened room, staring out at the street light not so very many yards from her window.

"Did I wake you?"

"No, I couldn't sleep."

"Sorry about this evening, dear."

Lexi flipped over on the bed. "Yeah, me too."

"I do think you're going to have to be a little nicer to Amanda. She is brand new to our home and—"

"She lied, Mother. She lied!" Lexi could hear her mother give a sad little sigh in the darkness.

"I know it's been difficult considering how quickly Amanda came to us and how little time we had to plan for this. I wanted to be more prepared and I wanted *you* to be more prepared. Maybe it would help if I told you a bit about Amanda's background."

"According to her, her background is great. She doesn't even know why she's here," Lexi said. "From what I can gather, she thinks this is a pretty dumb place to end up."

Mrs. Leighton shook her head. Lexi could see her silhouette in the dimness. "That might be how Amanda is talking about her situation, Lexi, but it's not how it actually was."

"What do you mean by that?"

"Amanda has had a very difficult background. She's seen a lot for a young girl. What she needs is some patience and love and consideration that she's never had before."

"But Amanda said—"

"There has to be a reason that she's staying with us and not her own family."

Lexi nodded grimly. "Probably because they wanted to give her away."

"Lexi," Mrs. Leighton warned, but Lexi could hear a little bit of a smile in her mother's voice.

"Well, it's probably true," Lexi said grumpily.

"Amanda's parents, according to Mrs. McNeil, are both alcoholics."

Lexi was silent for a long moment. "Oh."

"Neither have been able to hold good jobs for any length of time because of their alcohol problems, although they're both well-educated people."

"Is that enough to make Social Services find a new home for her?" Lexi wondered.

Mrs. Leighton shrugged her shoulders. "I'm not sure about those things, Lexi, all I know is that Amanda has run away from home a dozen times. Each time when both her parents were drinking."

The cold little shell around Lexi's heart began to thaw the tiniest bit.

"She's here because both her parents have agreed to enter treatment centers and there's no other family nearby with whom she could stay."

"So her parents are both in hospitals?"

Mrs. Leighton nodded. "Something like hospitals. Places where people go when they can't control the chemical substances they put into their bodies."

"And she's a runaway?" Lexi persisted.

Mrs. Leighton nodded. "All I ask is that you give her a chance, Lexi. I'm beginning to realize how much you resent the fact that I sprung this on you and I'm sorry for that, too. It was a bad choice on my part. Now that Amanda is here, we have to do everything within our power to make her feel loved and at home and welcome."

Lexi was already feeling very humbled. Perhaps she'd been unfair to Amanda. Mrs. Leighton laid a gentle hand on the top of Lexi's head and drew her palm along the soft, silky strands of her hair. "All I ask is that you try to understand Amanda, and that you try to understand what I'm doing. Even if she's frustrating or irritating or aggravating sometimes, remember, she hasn't had it easy."

"But we can't make up for all those years of her parents drinking," Lexi protested. "We can't do that at all."

Mrs. Leighton shook her head. "No, but we can show her that there are people that still know how to love." She sat down on her daughter's bed and put her arm around her shoulder. "And Lexi, I don't know of anyone who has a bigger heart or more a capacity to love than you. Don't shut her out, Lexi. Be patient. Give her a chance."

———

She would give her a chance, Lexi vowed later when she was alone. She'd try as hard as she could, no matter how it hurt. Perhaps it would be easier now that Lexi understood where Amanda was coming from. "Help, God," she petitioned. "Help me give Amanda the chance she needs so much."

Chapter Ten

Lexi had been working for nearly an hour when Mrs. Leighton and Amanda arrived at the veterinary clinic. She'd been particularly busy this afternoon since there was a mailing going out reminding clients to update their pets' rabies vaccinations. Lexi had just put a rubber band around the last stack of postcards when the door opened.

"Hello, dear. Busy?" Mrs. Leighton moved forward and brushed her lips across Lexi's forehead.

"Hi, Mom, I . . . oh, hello, Amanda." The blond girl hung back in the doorway, staring at the surroundings.

"Hullo."

"We've been shopping. Amanda said she needed a few things—socks, notebooks, shampoo—so we went to the mall. They have some wonderful clothes in for the new season, too. Don't they, Amanda."

"Uh huh."

"Anyway, Amanda found a darling skirt on sale. It's a little long, but I told her that you're an excellent seamstress and could easily hem it for her. You'll love

117

the fabric, Lexi, it's such bright colors and . . ."

Lexi stared at her mother, then Amanda, then her mother again.

Shopping! And they hadn't even asked her to join them?

"Say, Mom, I was thinking that I could get a pink blouse to go with that skirt. That would go with the belt, and I already have some pink shoes. . . ." Amanda emphasized her point with an enthusiastic waving of her hands.

Lexi blinked. *Mom?* Was Amanda calling Lexi's own mother *Mom?*

"That's a good idea, don't you think so, Lexi?" Mrs. Leighton asked, a big smile creasing her features.

"Yeah. Good."

Just then, Dr. Leighton walked into the room. He wore his white lab coat and his glasses rested on top of his head and he looked very important and professional. Though Mrs. Leighton and Amanda both turned his way, Lexi didn't move a muscle.

So that's how it was, Lexi thought bitterly. Amanda was moving in fast. First her posters and tapes, then shopping trips with Mrs. Leighton, now "Mom." An unpleasant, white-hot emotion began to seep into every fiber of Lexi's being.

"We'd better be going now," Mrs. Leighton was saying. "Amanda and I will have supper all ready for you two when you get home. Amanda says she has a fool-proof recipe for scalloped potatoes that she wants to demonstrate."

When they'd left, Lexi realized that her father was staring at her curiously.

"Are you all right, Lexi?"

Sure great. My life is falling apart.

"I don't know."

"You mustn't be jealous that your mother is spending some extra time with Amanda. I'm sure it's difficult for you, but you have to understand that Amanda needs some extra attention right now. It's our job to give it to her."

"Right."

There was nothing for Lexi to say. Her father was correct, of course. Amanda *had* come from a home where her parents drank and she felt compelled to run away. And now Amanda was in the process of ruining Lexi's happiness as well.

"You're kidding, right? I mean, your mother didn't actually take her shopping and leave you behind? Without even *telling* you they were going?" Jennifer mouthed the words in disbelief.

Lexi nodded morosely.

"That's cruel!" Binky huffed, her thin face pink and indignant. "I'll bet Amanda tricked her into going. She knew you had to work after school that night!"

"She probably waited until she knew you couldn't come along and then started moaning about needing stuff at the mall."

"And now you have to hem the skirt she bought? Sick!"

Egg had been quiet throughout this exchange among the girls, but now even he started to shake his head. "Maybe you're going to have to let Amanda know that she can't manipulate you and your mother like that."

Lexi held her hand helplessly in the air. "But how? Mom's 'mothering' hormones are pumping full steam ahead. She wants Amanda to know that even though she's had trouble at home it doesn't mean that she's not loveable. Besides, Amanda is like a different person around me than she is around my parents."

"Yeah, but Amanda is trying her hardest to push you and Ben into the background in your own home!" Jennifer pointed out.

"Maybe you should just try to understand where's she's coming from," Todd murmured. He'd been silent until now, his expression somber. "Then maybe she'd quit trying to push you out of the picture."

"Or maybe she should get even," Jennifer added with malicious glee. "Show her a thing or two!"

"Yeah, get even!" Binky rejoined. Her eyes narrowed. "Do something really mean and let her see what it feels like!"

Jennifer and Binky spent the next two minutes painting worst-case scenarios in which Amanda was the victim. Finally Lexi held up her hand.

"Listen, guys, revenge sounds great, but I can't. Just because Amanda is being rotten to me doesn't mean I have the right to be rotten back." She'd read it in the Bible last night.

> You have heard that it was said, "An eye for an eye and a tooth for a tooth. But I say to you, Do not resist one who is evil. But if any one strikes you on the right cheek, turn to him the other one also; and if any one would sue you and take your coat, let

him have your cloak as well; and if any one forces
you to go one mile, go with him two miles.

Those were hard words, Lexi had mused. Even
Todd didn't realize how Amanda was jerking her
around these days—especially since she felt like
she'd already gone the second mile with Amanda.
Still, God's Word had been awfully specific on han-
dling people like her.

"I guess I'll just have to ride this out and keep on
being nice to her."

Todd nodded approvingly. "I think Lexi is right.
She should 'rise above it.' That's what my mother
always says. Pretend it's not happening. Ignore it.
She'll get the message eventually."

———————

But "rising above" the antics Amanda was pulling was easier said than done. With every passing
day, Amanda was getting on Lexi's nerves more and
more.

What made it so much worse was that Minda had
gotten into the act.

Lexi was putting her books into her locker when
Amanda and Minda sauntered up to her.

"Lexi, will you tell Mom that I'll be home late
tonight?" Amanda asked.

Lexi looked up sharply. She couldn't get used to
Amanda calling her own mother "Mom."

"Sure, but she'll ask when you plan to be home."

"I'm having a little get-together after school,"
Minda explained. "Hi-Fives, mostly. And Amanda."

"I should be home by suppertime."

"I thought it was your turn to help with supper

tonight," Lexi reminded her.

"Oh, you can do that for me. Mom won't mind too much."

Maybe not, but I will. Not that you care about that.

"The Hi-Fives just love Amanda," Minda pointed out gleefully. "It's not everyone they like, you know."

Lexi knew that all too well. She was on their "dislike list" and had been ever since she refused to go through with their unfair initiation. She also knew that Minda's friendship with Amanda was purely a ploy on Minda's part to get under Lexi's skin. If Amanda and Lexi had been on more friendly terms, Minda wouldn't have bothered with Amanda at all.

Still, that knowledge didn't comfort Lexi as she watched Amanda and Minda stroll away together.

Things were getting out of hand. Lexi was beginning to feel like an outsider in her own home. She was working so many nights at her father's office that she hardly had time to spend with Jennifer and Binky. Todd was sympathetic toward her situation with Amanda, but he didn't really understand it because Amanda was always so syrupy sweet around him. Lexi couldn't understand why he didn't get cavities just talking to her.

She glanced down the empty hallway. Everyone had gone. A rush of misery engulfed her.

"I'm being pushed out of everything," she muttered to herself. "Everything. And nobody understands or sees it happening. Not Mom and Dad, not Todd. . . ." her voice drifted away before she added, ". . . not even God." Lexi felt as empty and deserted as the hallway she stood in.

With a deep sigh, Lexi picked up her backpack

and walked toward the music room. She'd skipped work today to practice her solo for the Emerald Tones. She loved being in the music room. That was the one place that Amanda never came.

Amanda claimed she couldn't sing and wasn't interested in trying. No doubt it didn't seem interesting or flashy enough. Lexi was glad. The music room had become her one safe haven in the storm her life had become.

"Hello, Lexi, ready to practice?" Mrs. Waverly was sitting at the baby grand. Her hair was sprouting pencils and she was smiling. It occurred to Lexi that Mrs. Waverly was actually rather pretty.

Lexi nodded and dropped her bag to the floor.

"How's the solo coming?"

"Okay, I guess. I've had trouble with a couple spots."

"Well, whenever you do, just come right in and we'll work on them. I can always take a little extra time for you, Lexi."

That did it. That single, concerned, affectionate statement turned on the waterworks that had been stored up inside Lexi for days. It was what Lexi had been waiting to hear from someone, anyone, since Amanda had arrived to disrupt her life. *I can always take a little extra time for you, Lexi.*

Lexi started to cry.

She didn't cry quietly or in ladylike whimpers but in great, gulping sobs that shook her entire body and alarmed both Lexi and Mrs. Waverly.

In a single, quick move, Mrs. Waverly moved from the piano to put her arms around Lexi.

"There, there. It can't be all that bad. My goodness, Lexi, can you tell me what's wrong?" As she spoke Mrs. Waverly led Lexi toward her private office. Inside, she pulled a curtain across the window that faced the music room and locked the door.

She helped Lexi into a chair, poured a glass of water from the pitcher on her desk and handed it to the crying girl. Finally, she perched on the edge of the desk.

"What's wrong, Lexi? You can tell me."

Lexi believed she could. The story of her mother, the foster parenting idea and Amanda came pouring out in a choked and hiccuping litany.

Mrs. Waverly did not interrupt until Lexi was finished.

"I know I'm just being selfish and jealous, Mrs. Waverly. I know that Amanda comes from a bad place and that my mother is right. I should be glad to share with her . . . but I'm not!"

"Of course you aren't!"

That frank statement got Lexi's attention. "You don't think I'm bad?"

"Not a bit. What I think you are is *normal*."

Lexi snuffled, a flicker of hope lighting within her. "I am?"

"Absolutely. What teenage girl wouldn't be jealous if all of a sudden she had to share everything—including her parents—with another girl! And it's especially hard because Amanda seems to be as clinging and proprietorial of your mother as you are."

"You make it sound like it's okay to feel this way."

Mrs. Waverly smiled and pulled up a chair to sit

across from Lexi. "I'd like to tell you my story, if you don't mind."

Lexi shook her head.

"My husband and I were foster parents once."

"You were?"

"Oh, yes. For about three years, before I went back to teaching full time." Mrs. Waverly smiled. "I like children. While I wasn't teaching, I just couldn't see my life without them, so we entered the foster parent program."

"Just like my folks?"

"Exactly. It's a wonderful program. There are so many children that need a 'stopping off' place for a time because their home lives are disrupted. You know, Lexi, if Amanda's home life were decent at all, she wouldn't be living with you."

"I know that. That's what makes it so much worse. I'm jealous of someone who's not nearly as lucky as me—and then I feel guilty about it!"

"Have you talked to your mother about how you feel?"

Lexi shook her head. "She's so concerned about Amanda adjusting to us that I think she's forgotten we need to adjust to her!" Lexi's lips curled down at the corners. "Amanda certainly has it nice at our house. She'd think it was perfect if *I* didn't live there!"

Mrs. Waverly gave a tight smile. "Perhaps it would help if you could understand Amanda a little better?"

Lexi's shoulders sank. "I don't know how I'd do that."

"Maybe I can help you. I don't know Amanda very

well, but I have an idea how her mind works."

"You do?"

"Put yourself in her shoes for a moment. Her parents are both in alcohol treatment centers. She's all alone in the world for the time being. There are no relatives who will take her in. She's scared. What if her parents don't come back? What if they *do* come back and they haven't quit drinking?"

"I didn't think of it like that. . . ."

"Then she comes to the Leighton household. There's a pretty girl named Lexi there who has two beautiful, loving parents and a little brother. Lexi seems to have everything—and Amanda has nothing. She doesn't even have a radio or cassettes to call her own."

"But—"

"Wouldn't *you* be jealous of a girl who had everything you wanted? Wouldn't you resent the fact that some people are so lucky while others—like herself—are so *unlucky*?"

"I suppose. . . ."

"Wouldn't you want to pretend—even for a little while—that the mother in this family is *your* mother?"

"Maybe, but—"

"And wouldn't you even wish that the girl in the family were gone? That this family had a place in it for you?"

Lexi remained silent.

"It's my guess that Amanda resents you, Lexi. She's just as jealous of you as you are of her. And, from my experience with foster kids, I'm also guessing that Amanda is desperately longing for her own mother—and clinging to yours as a replacement."

"But she's *my* mother!"

Mrs. Waverly nodded. "Of course she is. Your mother knows that. But your mother also knows how insecure Amanda is right now. She realizes that she's probably got a very worried, unstable girl on her hands. And," Mrs. Waverly gently wiped a stray lock of hair from Lexi's forehead, "she also knows that her own daughter is very secure and stable and bright. She's assuming you can handle this situation and has no idea whatsoever about how you feel."

Lexi found herself nodding. Everything Mrs. Waverly said made sense.

"But what do I do now?" Lexi wondered, her voice quivering.

Mrs. Waverly sat back and considered the question. "Well, teacher that I am, I always like a plan."

"A plan?"

"A three-part plan."

"Oh?"

Mrs. Waverly smiled. "Let me tell you what I'd do. Then you can decide for yourself." She folded her hands in her lap. "First of all, because I know how important your faith is to you, Lexi, I'd pray. Pray for help to like Amanda in spite of what she is and does."

"Sort of like praying for your enemies?"

"*Exactly* like praying for your enemies."

"Then what?"

"Then I'd start a little project of my own. I'd try to make Amanda feel as loved by you as she does by your mother."

"Me?"

"Show her that having a loving, caring friend is important too. Show her that affection will get her farther than resentment."

"That's harder than praying."

"Taking action on your prayers always is, but it's important."

"So what's the third step?"

"Tell your mother how you've been feeling."

"But—"

"Do it sometime when Amanda isn't around. Do it in a nonthreatening way. Show your mom you aren't angry—just hurt and confused. Tell her you need help. No mom will turn that away."

Lexi thought about Mrs. Waverly's words for a long moment. They sounded right and smart and sensible. She wished she'd thought of them herself.

"Do I have to practice my song today?" she finally asked. "My voice is a little weak."

"Not today."

"Maybe I should be going home, then." Lexi smiled. "I have some things to do—three things."

Mrs. Waverly smiled. "And I'll be praying, too."

When Lexi left the music room, both her heart and her step were lighter.

At least now she had a plan of action.

Chapter Eleven

When Lexi awoke the next morning, a single, urgent thought was running through her mind.

Step one. Pray for her.

Lexi flung herself backward on the pillows and stared at the ceiling. Sometimes she liked to pray this way, looking upward as if she could see beyond the ceiling, beyond the rooftop, beyond the clouds. It allowed her mind to roam free, to talk to God as a friend. It was even easier to talk to God than it was to Jennifer and Binky. Maybe it was because Lexi knew He *always* listened.

"Good morning, Father," she began. "I need to talk to you about the plan Mrs. Waverly gave me for dealing with Amanda. I'm beginning to understand that she's got lots of problems, Lord. Lots more than I can probably ever imagine. And you know them better than I ever will. Help her to deal with her troubles in the right way, Lord—not by being mean and spiteful. And I pray for her parents because they both have alcohol problems. Heal them and send them back to Amanda so she can have a family again.

Oh, and by the way, Lord, help me to be patient with her. Maybe I can help her if You'll show me how. . . ."

Lexi was startled when her father knocked on her bedroom door.

"Up yet, Lexi? Shower is free."

"Ah, yeah, thanks, Dad."

She got up feeling better than she had in days. Amanda was too big a burden for her to carry alone. Mrs. Waverly had made her see that. Now she had two people helping her carry the load, her music teacher and, most importantly, God.

Lexi was whistling when she stepped out of the shower. It didn't even matter that Amanda had used most of the hot water and left her a shower that was practically tepid. Then Lexi heard Amanda's voice in the hallway. She was scolding Ben.

"Move it, Kid, breakfast is ready and I don't want to be late for school."

Lexi could hear Ben's plaintive voice trying to defend himself. "Ben's hurrying. I am."

A knot tied itself around her heart. Suddenly step two loomed before Lexi.

How was she supposed to love Amanda when Amanda could act so callously? How was she supposed to show Amanda that there was enough love in this family to go around? Enough so that no one should have to be shortchanged? And how was she supposed to love when it was such a tiny, ungerminated seed in her heart?

A chance to show her love for Amanda came along sooner than Lexi had anticipated. Though she'd only gotten glimpses of Amanda in the hallway at school, Lexi knew that something was troubling her.

Amanda often appeared sullen or pouty. Today, she was looking downright miserable.

Between classes, Lexi had noticed Amanda and Minda having a heart-to-heart conversation outside the Biology classroom. Amanda was gesturing angrily, her eyebrows furrowing into a line across her flashing brown eyes. Minda, in response to whatever Amanda was saying, was simply shrugging her shoulders and looking slightly bored. Curious, Lexi had thought to herself, but she didn't have time to dwell on what Amanda and Minda might be talking about. Her own class was about to start.

At noon, as Lexi stood in front of her locker, putting away her books, Amanda came storming up next to her. She threw open her own locker, flung a notebook and math text onto the floor of the locker and slammed it shut with such force that the metal shuttered and creaked.

Lexi, mentally reminding herself of step two, turned to Amanda and said sympathetically, "Bad day?"

Amanda looked up sharply, her eyes flashing. "What's it to you?"

Lexi gave a small shrug. "Nothing, I guess. I just hate to see anyone looking so upset."

Amanda's eyes flickered as she stared at Lexi. "I don't see why you're concerned if I'm upset or not."

Lexi gave a small smile. "No, you probably don't, but I am." Then she added impulsively, "Want to talk about it?"

Lexi wished later that she had a picture of the look of surprise on Amanda's features.

"Not really."

Then an idea struck Lexi. This had something to do with the strange conversation she had seen Amanda and Minda having in the hallway. Lexi was sure of it.

"Trouble with Minda?" she asked mildly.

Amanda's response was completely unexpected. Large, unhappy tears welled in her eyes and her shoulders convulsed in misery. "She said I couldn't be a High-Five because I'm not going to be staying at the Cedar River High School."

Amanda was gullible to have believed that she'd be considered for the High-Fives, Lexi knew, but she was wise enough not to say it. Minda had dumped her. It had only been a matter of time before that would happen. Only Amanda had been naive enough to think that Minda's offer of friendship had been a sincere one.

"She doesn't even want me eating lunch with the High-Fives anymore," Amanda choked out. "She says they have business to discuss. Private club business."

Don't put all your eggs in one basket, Lexi thought to herself. Her father liked to say that and she never had quite understood what it meant, but now she did. It was like Amanda, counting on only one friend. When that friend turned sour, everything was lost.

"I'm going to lunch right now," Lexi said. "Would you like to join me?"

"You? Just you?"

"Well, Egg and Binky will be there, and Jennifer for sure. But they won't mind if you eat with us."

"Why? Why would you ask me to join you?" Amanda's voice was suspicious and her eyes narrow.

"Why not?" Lexi responded.

"Your friends don't like me," Amanda pointed out matter-of-factly. "And I've never exactly said that I like them either."

Lexi shrugged. "It's up to you. I'm going now and you're welcome to come."

With a puzzled expression on her face, Amanda followed Lexi down the hall and through the cafeteria line. When they reached the table where Egg and Jennifer were sitting, they were greeted by surprised expressions.

"Amanda's going to eat with us today," Lexi explained. "I hope that's all right with you guys."

Egg's head bobbed mechanically.

Jennifer, who was not so willing to welcome an enemy into their camp, merely stared at Lexi with questioning eyes.

Binky came rushing up to the foursome. "Sorry I'm late. I thought we were never going to get out of class. I . . . oh, hello, Amanda." The bright light went out of her eyes and Binky became wary.

It was blatantly obvious that none of Lexi's friends were pleased to see Amanda. Still, Lexi made every effort to include her in the conversation.

When the topic of summer jobs came up and Egg promptly began to complain that he didn't know what he'd be doing to earn money for the coming summer, Lexi turned to Amanda. "Have you ever had a summer job, Amanda?"

Amanda, who had been silent through the entire meal, nodded briefly.

"What was it?" Lexi persisted.

Amanda dropped her chin into the collar of her

blouse. "A mime," she mumbled.

"A what?" Lexi asked.

"A mime," Amanda raised her eyes. "You know, like a clown—an actor who doesn't speak. A mime."

"You were a mime?" Binky echoed. "What does a mime do?"

Suddenly, all of the attention which had been hostile, was now simply curious and focused on Amanda.

"I was a mime in a park. I wore a black suit and white gloves and painted my face and wore a black hat and I did miming."

"And you got paid for it?"

Amanda nodded. "We'd put out hats and the people in the park would throw money to us. There were street musicians and clowns and mimes and people giving lessons on how to make stained glass and all sorts of crafts. It was sort of like working at a park fair for a summer."

"That's neat," Jennifer gasped. "How'd you get a job like that?"

A half smile crept onto her lips. "I had to go to the park board and get interviewed. I thought that maybe I could work planting flowers or something, but all those jobs were taken. The guy at the desk said that the only openings left were for entertainers. So, I applied."

"Where did you learn to be a mime?" Egg wondered.

"I read some books. I watched some tapes. It isn't too hard. Not really. Watch." Her eyes flickered and suddenly her face became impassive. She looked to the right and to the left and to the right again, then held up her right hand, palm outward, just to the right of her face. It was as if there were a barrier there. She pushed on it, but her hand did not give. She did the same in front of her face and to the other side. Right there, before their very eyes, it seemed that Amanda had transformed herself into a character who was trapped in a little glass box. The harder she pushed on the glass and the more she strained, the less likely it seemed that she would get out of the glass. Then suddenly, she dropped her hands to her lap and laughed.

"See? Could you tell what I was doing?"

"You looked like you were trapped inside something."

"Yeah, like a fish in an aquarium," Egg added.

"That's great," Jennifer enthused. "Could you teach me to do that?"

Amanda's eyebrows rose in surprise. "Well, I suppose. It's not hard. I learned it."

Lexi laughed and clapped her hands. "I think it's great. I think she should teach all of us. Don't you?"

Amanda swiveled to stare at Lexi in disbelief. "You're kidding, right?"

"No, not at all. I think that would be fun to learn. Don't you, guys?" Lexi turned to her friends who all nodded.

"Maybe Egg could get up a mime troop for the summer and then he wouldn't have to worry about finding a job."

"That's all we need," Binky interjected. "My brother Egg spearheading a group of clowns. Can you imagine what the park system would be like at the end of the summer?"

Everyone began to laugh. The conversation

drifted naturally onto other things. Still, at the end of the meal, when all the plates and trays had been cleared away, Amanda was still beside Lexi giving her a strange "what's up" sort of look.

Rather than be offended by the suspicious glances, Lexi smiled into Amanda's face. "It was nice having lunch with you today. Thanks for joining us. I'd better go now or I'll be late for class." With that, Lexi walked off, shoulders square, head held high. She'd put step two into action. Would it help?

Each time Lexi caught a glimpse of Amanda in a classroom or hallway, Amanda was staring at her as if to say "What's with you? What's going on?" The confusion on Amanda's face would have been amusing had Lexi not been so intent on making up for the kindness she'd withheld from the girl for so long.

After school, Lexi caught up with Amanda in the hallway. "I'm going to Dad's office. Would you like to come along? There's the cutest pair of little monkeys in the back right now. They're so sweet and so lovable and they need to be played with."

Amanda shook her head. "No, I don't think so. I've got a lot of studying to do tonight." Then, remembering who she was and that she didn't like this Lexi person at all, she added, "Anyway, I think it's dumb to play with monkeys."

Rather than make a sharp retort, Lexi nodded. "It probably is, but they're awfully cute. See you later."

She wouldn't let Amanda make her angry, Lexi told herself as she walked away. She wouldn't. She couldn't. It had become far too important to her that Amanda know that she really could care.

The next afternoon, after Phy. Ed., Lexi unintentionally stumbled onto a scene between Minda and Amanda. Most of the girls had already showered and left when Lexi entered the locker room to pick up the towel she'd forgotten the previous hour. As she stooped to retrieve the soggy towel, she could hear two girls talking at the sinks around the corner from the showers.

"But, I don't see why," one voice was saying.

"That's your problem, you just don't see," the other retorted nastily. "I can't give you anymore hints. I'm just gonna have to say it outright. The High-Fives discussed it and they don't want you to join them for lunch anymore."

"But everyone seemed so friendly," the first voice protested.

"Well, things aren't always as they seem. Now, you've just got to get it through your head. They don't want you."

Lexi froze in her tracks. That was Amanda's voice she was hearing on the other side of the wall. Amanda's and Minda's.

"But I'll do anything you want," Amanda pleaded.

Minda gave a brittle laugh. "Sorry. There's nothing you can do. The High-Fives are very selective. You just don't fit."

"Is it because I'm a foster kid?" Amanda asked, her voice trembling.

"That doesn't help," Minda admitted truthfully.

"That's not my fault," Amanda protested.

"No one said it was. Hey, there must be a dozen other groups at school that you could hang out with."

"But I want to be with you."

Lexi winced. Amanda had resorted to begging.

Minda's brittle laugh filled the air again. "Yeah? I think that's only because Lexi Leighton isn't in the group. You're afraid that nobody else will want to hang out with you except for Lexi and her friends. Well . . ." and Lexi could just imagine Minda giving a careless shrug, "that's too bad. The High-Fives voted. Sorry."

Lexi dodged into one of the bathroom stalls just as Minda came around the corner, humming under her breath. A moment later, she could hear snuffling and the sound of soft sobs in the other room. Stealthily, Lexi opened the stall door and slipped out. She peeked around the corner. Amanda was standing at the sink, tears streaming down her face.

"Amanda?" Lexi said.

Amanda spun around, startled. "What are you doing here?" She tried to wipe away the tell-tale tears with the back of her hand.

"I came to pick up my towel and I overheard," Lexi tipped her head toward the door through which Minda had gone.

"You were eavesdropping?" Amanda said angrily. "How dare you?"

"I wasn't eavesdropping," Lexi corrected. "I came for my towel and I overheard what the two of you were talking about. I'm sorry, Amanda."

Amanda stared at her through red-rimmed eyes. "You're sorry? What for? What do you care?"

"I'm sorry that Minda hurt you. She's pretty good at that. She's had lots of practice. I know that there's a nice person in there somewhere, but it just doesn't come out very often," Lexi tried to form a weak smile.

Amanda stared at her suspiciously. "What's gotten into you? You're feeling sorry for me? You're apologizing for Minda? It doesn't make any sense, Lexi. You hate me. I know you do. You've hated me ever since the day I came to live at your house."

Lexi wanted to deny it, but at least a portion of what Amanda said was true. She hadn't been happy to have the girl arrive. It was only the last few days that made her see that her response had been all wrong and needed to be corrected.

"I might not have been happy when you came," Lexi said honestly. "But I've changed. I'm glad you're living with us now."

Amanda looked at her doubtfully, as if she'd just claimed she could fly. "Yeah? And what caused this big transformation? Guilt? Did your mother threaten you?"

Lexi bit back a retort. Amanda was just trying to bait her; trying to make her angry. She was certainly doing an excellent job.

"Amanda, I know that you came to our house because your own house wasn't a good place to stay in right now and that you didn't need people who disliked you or resented your being there. You need people who would welcome you and grow to be fond of you."

"So that's what you think, Freud," Amanda said sarcastically. "Very impressive."

"I know you don't want to listen to what I have to say, and I really don't blame you, but I just want you to know that I'd like to be your friend. I understand why you're staying at our house, and I'm glad that you get along so well with my mother."

"Thanks for nothing. Just what I needed now, your friendship."

"Is it that unimportant to you, Amanda?" Lexi inquired somberly.

"I don't need friends. I don't need anyone."

"Everybody needs someone," Lexi protested.

Amanda shook her head violently. "Not me. I thought Minda was being sincere. I thought she really liked me and look what happened. The same thing will happen all over again. First you'll decide to be nice to me and then you'll dump me, too. Everyone does. Even my parents."

As soon as the words were out of her mouth, Lexi could tell Amanda regretted them. It had been too much of an admission of the fear she carried inside her.

"We won't dump you, and your parents didn't—"

But Amanda would not allow her to finish. Instead, she gathered up her brush and hair spray, shoved them into her bag and raced past Lexi toward the door. "I don't want to hear this. I don't believe you mean it. No one wants me. Not you—not anyone. And I don't care. Now just go away and leave me alone."

———

Leaving Amanda alone was easier said than done, Lexi decided at supper that night. As they sat across the dinner table from each other, Amanda shot Lexi a series of daggered looks.

Oh great, Lexi thought to herself. *Instead of making things better, instead of showing Amanda that I'd like to accept her and to love her, all I've done is teach her that I can interfere and embarrass her by having overheard the conversation she'd had with Minda.*

"Would you girls do the dishes tonight?" Mrs. Leighton inquired pleasantly, trying to ignore the cold war going on between the two girls at the table.

"Sure, Mom—" Lexi began.

"I'll do it," Amanda interrupted. Everyone stared at her. "I'll do the dishes. Alone. That's the way I want to do them."

The message was perfectly clear. Amanda would rather spend an extra half hour in the kitchen than have to be with Lexi.

Lexi lowered her eyes and refused to look at her mother. She knew what was there. Mrs. Leighton was always giving Lexi accusing stares as if to ask "What did you say to her? What have you done to make her so angry?" Now Lexi had both Amanda and her mother to avoid for the rest of the evening.

Even Mr. Leighton announced just before bedtime, "It's chilly in here, isn't it?"

"Why, I just turned the heat up, dear," Mrs. Leighton began.

Mr. Leighton shook his head. "That's not what I meant. I didn't mean it was cold. I meant it was chilly. I think Amanda and Lexi know what I'm talking about."

Before her father could pursue the conversation, Lexi jumped up from her chair and planted a kiss on his cheek. "Bedtime, Pops," she said with a false cheerfulness. "I think I'd better say good-night."

Unwillingly, Mr. Leighton let her go and Lexi escaped into the confines of her bedroom. *Great,* she thought sarcastically to herself, *step two is working out just dandy*. She had set out to show Amanda that she liked her and they were speaking even less than they were before. "Maybe I'll have to go back to step one for awhile," Lexi told herself as she reached for her Bible. "Maybe step two should be implemented with a little more prayer."

The next morning when Mr. Leighton offered Amanda and Lexi a ride to school, Lexi shook her head. "I'm not quite ready yet, Dad. You and Amanda go on ahead. I'll take my bike."

Her father looked surprised, but didn't argue. "All right then, we'll see you after school."

After they'd gone, Mrs. Leighton poured herself a second cup of coffee and sat down at the kitchen table. She curled her legs beneath her and cupped her chin in her hand and stared at her daughter. It occurred to Lexi that her mother was very young and pretty looking. Too young to have teenage girls, especially ones with the problems that she and Amanda seemed to be facing.

"Since I know very well you're ready for school, I take it you have something to say to me," Mrs. Leighton said with a smile. "You're not a very good liar, Lexi."

Lexi returned the grin. "I've never tried to be."

"Well, thank goodness for that," her mother chuckled. "So, tell me, what is it?"

Lexi sank into the chair across from her mother. "We have to talk, Mom. About Amanda."

A frown flittered across Mrs. Leighton's features.

"You and Amanda don't get along very well, do you?"

Lexi shook her head. "Amanda and I don't get along at all."

"And I had such high hopes . . ." Mrs. Leighton said sadly. "I really thought that our house would be good for Amanda—and good for you, too, since you've never had a sister."

Lexi broke in. "She isn't my sister, Mom, and she never can be. You mustn't expect us to try." Lexi sighed. "But I have been trying to be nice to her. Especially lately. But even that doesn't seem to be working."

"Oh?" Mrs. Leighton said. "Tell me."

And the whole story came pouring out about Lexi's unhappiness at her mother's idea of becoming foster parents; about her initial shock and surprise when Amanda arrived so quickly on their doorstep; about the multiple personalities that Amanda seemed to have—nice one moment and snotty the next. About the jealousy she felt when Amanda took Mrs. Leighton's time and about the guilt that followed jealousy. She also told her that she'd realized how very much she had and how little she was willing to share.

Then, hard as it was to tell, Lexi explained what had happened in the music room with Mrs. Waverly. She talked about the three step plan that Mrs. Waverly had suggested she use to turn Amanda around and how miserably it was failing. All the while Lexi talked, her mother remained silent.

After Lexi explained the last disagreement that she and Amanda had had in the locker room, Mrs. Leighton straightened her shoulders and stared directly into her daughter's eyes. "Lexi, I had no idea."

"I know you didn't, Mom. I suppose that's partly my fault. But you were so excited about helping someone, about doing good."

"Doing good? When it ultimately hurts my family and makes them miserable and unhappy?" Mrs. Leighton shook her head. "It's all wrong if that's what happens, Lexi."

"Well, it wouldn't need to happen," Lexi said hopefully. "If I could just get Amanda to realize that I don't hate her; that I don't want to hate her; that I want to treat her with kindness and respect. But, every time I do or say something that I think is nice, Amanda rejects it immediately. It's as if she won't believe me." Lexi sighed. "I suppose she's been lied to so many times that she's learned to not trust anyone."

Mrs. Leighton nodded thoughtfully. "I think something is beginning to happen that the Social Worker told me to expect."

"Oh?" Lexi looked up with interest. "What was that?"

"Amanda's been shifted in and out of several foster homes while her parents have been trying to solve their problems. Each time, just as she's gotten accustomed to the new place she's living, they've had to pull her out and put her back in her own home because her parents think they're ready to handle her again. She's afraid to get close to anyone, Lexi. Even if she desperately wanted you for a friend, she'd feel that it was too risky to develop that friendship. After all, she has no idea how long she'll be with us, either."

"So she wants to reject us? That way it won't hurt so much when they take her away?"

Mrs. Leighton nodded. "Something like that."

Lexi stared out the window toward the blue sky. "It's so complicated," she murmured.

"That it is." Mrs. Leighton uncurled her legs and stood up. "And I had no idea how complicated your problems were, Lexi. I apologize. In my enthusiasm for making Amanda feel at home, I did just the opposite for you. I made you feel pushed and twisted right out of your place in this family. I must admit, I have a lot to learn about becoming a foster parent."

"You're a great parent," Lexi protested. "One of the best. If Amanda had been born into our family, she'd be a great kid, too," Lexi smiled impishly. "Just like me."

Mrs. Leighton laughed and threw her arms around her daughter. "Exactly right, Lexi, she'd be a great kid—just like you. I'm glad we had this talk. Now I'll know that I need to be a little more sensitive to your needs."

"And what about Amanda?" Lexi asked.

"We'll love her, even if she acts like she doesn't want to be loved," Mrs. Leighton said with a sad smile. "And we'll pray things will work out for her."

Lexi nodded. "Back to step one again." She was seeing now that that prayer step was of primary importance in what became of Amanda's life.

Chapter Twelve

One step forward, two steps back.

That was how Lexi's attempts to show Amanda that she truly did care for her seemed to progress. Amanda still mistrusted and resented her, but she wasn't so verbal about it now. Sometimes, when she let her guard down, she actually seemed to like Lexi. It was a little like hammering away at a stone wall with a toy hammer. There was never much visible progress.

Still, Amanda willingly came to sit with Lexi and her friends at lunch. She'd quit attempting to flirt with Todd and accepted the fact that his interest was only in Lexi. Amanda had even agreed to study with Egg one night at the public library. Even Binky and Jennifer had quit plotting to rid themselves—and Lexi—of her.

Lexi and Amanda were sitting on the floor of Lexi's bedroom doing homework and sharing a bowl of popcorn when Amanda dropped her bombshell.

"You're the first friend I've ever had."

Lexi looked up from her English composition paper in astonishment. Could that be *Amanda* speaking?

"What?"

"You're the first friend. *Real* friend, that is, that I've ever had."

"I . . . ah . . . oh!"

Amanda smiled sadly. "You didn't know I thought of you as my friend, did you?"

Lexi shook her head. "Most of the time I thought you hated me."

Amanda's shoulders drooped and her head hung low. "I know. I'm sorry. I've been really rotten to you."

Lexi shrugged. "It's okay, I guess. Those first few days I wasn't very glad to have you here, either."

"But you changed."

"I'm glad you noticed."

"This is the best foster home I've been in," Amanda confided. She rarely talked of her past.

"Have you been in many?"

"Too many. Most of them only for a few days, though. This is the longest I've stayed in one place. Usually my mom and dad have tried to get me back right away. They've never completed an entire alcohol treatment program before."

"So, maybe this time, when they get out, things will be better."

"Maybe." Amanda looked fifty years older than her years as she said that, Lexi noticed. Perhaps that was the look that came from being disappointed so many times in the past.

"When do you think they'll be home again?"

"How long have I been here?" Amanda wondered.

"Almost six weeks."

A frown flickered across her features. "Soon then."

Perhaps, Lexi thought later, Amanda had an instinct for that sort of thing, or perhaps she knew that the call would be coming and was trying to prepare herself for it. Neither of them were really surprised when Mrs. Leighton stepped into the room to impart her news.

"May I come in?"

"Sure. We're almost done. Popcorn?"

"No, thanks. I'm not hungry."

Lexi looked sharply at her mother. She knew immediately that something was wrong.

"What is it, Mom?"

Amanda glanced up, too. Her eyes grew wary.

"Anna McNeil called today."

Lexi noticed Amanda's hand tighten around her pencil.

"Amanda, your parents will be coming out of treatment soon. They'd like you to move back home with them. Mrs. McNeil is coming tomorrow to discuss it with you."

"Oh, yeah?" Amanda said casually, as if she'd just heard a weather report. "Okay."

"Is that all? Just 'okay'?" Lexi asked.

Amanda slid her bare toes into her slippers and stretched theatrically. "Listen, I'm really whipped. I think I'll go to bed now."

Lexi watched in amazement as Amanda sauntered out the door as though nothing had happened. What was wrong with that girl? Didn't she have any feelings at all?

Lexi rushed angrily through her nightly ritual of

face-washing and toothbrushing. Hadn't her family meant any more to Amanda than a glorified hotel? She was still insulted as she stomped down the hall to her room, but was stopped by the sound of muffled sobs coming from Amanda's bedroom.

Lexi paused a moment before knocking softly on the door. "Amanda?"

"Go away."

"I don't think so." Lexi opened the door a crack and decided that she could be just as stubborn as Amanda if she needed to be.

"Go away, I said!"

"Want to talk about it?"

"Are you going away?"

"No."

"Then I suppose you can come in."

Lexi entered the room and perched on the corner of Amanda's bed. "When Mom told you that you'd be leaving, I thought you didn't care. At least, that's how you acted."

"I *shouldn't* care, but I guess I do."

There was a long moment of silence between them before Amanda continued. "It's starting all over again, Lexi."

"What is?"

"This moving around. I never stay in one place."

"But you're going home to your parents!"

"Do you think it will last?" she asked in anguish. "How long do you think they'll stay sober?"

"They've never had this much treatment before, have they?"

"No."

"Then you've got to give them a chance. Maybe

this time will be the one that works."

"I'm so scared, Lexi." Amanda crouched at the head of the bed like a frightened little animal who quivered at the sounds of a hunter.

Lexi moved toward the girl with her arms extended and wrapped them around Amanda as she soothed, "It will be okay this time. You have to believe that. They stuck it out."

It occurred to Lexi at that moment, as she and Amanda clung to each other in the tiny guest room of the Leighton household, that she actually *did* love this ... intruder ... who'd disrupted their lives so immensely. She loved her. Without qualification. Without reservation. Just as she might love a long-lost sister now found.

Then it struck Lexi that she, too, was trembling. This love she felt wasn't springing from her own resources but from God's. Step one—all those prayers—was working.

"I'll pray for you, Amanda, and for your parents. We all will."

Amanda pulled away slightly. "That's how you managed to stand me, wasn't it? By praying?"

Lexi gave a weak smile. "Yes. It was difficult for me to manage on my own."

Amanda gave her a quick hug and Lexi saw a smile cross her face.

"Well, if God can manage that, maybe He *can* keep my parents sober!"

———

She was leaving.

Mr. and Mrs. Leighton stood on the front porch

visiting with Anna McNeil, the social worker, while Lexi and Amanda attempted to make uncomfortable small talk. Ben, whose attitude toward Amanda had thawed as soon as she'd started being kind to him, was clinging to her hand.

As Amanda bent to talk to Ben, Lexi studied her.

She looked young and scared, Lexi realized. How could she have ever seemed such a big threat? Before she could pursue the thought, voices called to her.

"She isn't gone yet, is she?"

"We didn't miss her. . . ."

"Oh, hi! There you are."

Egg, Binky and Jennifer trooped up the sidewalk to the house.

"We wanted to say goodbye," Binky explained.

"And we were afraid we'd miss you!" Jennifer's eyes sparkled. "Egg has something he wants to give you."

Amanda looked started. "To me?"

Egg shuffled his feet against the pavement and flushed the color of freshly cooked beets. He drug his hand out from behind his back. Clutched in it was a single rose.

"Why, Egg!"

"We think he's got a crush on you," Binky explained cheerfully.

Egg glowered at his sister.

"And if you were staying much longer, he'd get over Minda Hannaford and start being crazy about you," Jennifer concluded.

"She's a good study partner," Egg said with as much dignity as he could muster. "Right?"

Amanda buried her nose in the flower and sniffed

deeply. Then she smiled dreamily up at Egg. "Oh, Egg, you're so sweet . . ."

Lexi and Jennifer exchanged a glance. Binky giggled. The spell was broken.

"Todd is working, but he said to tell you goodbye and good luck," Jennifer said. "Where are you going, anyway?"

Amanda sighed. "My parents have decided that the best thing for us would be a fresh start. My father has a job out of state."

"So you won't be back to visit?"

"Not for a while." Amanda smiled. "But I can write to you."

"Great! I love pen-pals. Do you have my address?"

"Lexi gave me everything I need. I'd planned to write to you all and apologize for being such a jerk while I was here. . . ."

Jennifer grinned. "Hey! I'm a jerk sometimes, too! Don't worry about it!"

"Time to go, Amanda," Mrs. MacNeil announced. "Have you got everything?"

Amanda looked from Lexi to the others and then down at the rose. "Everything I need."

Before she could think about it, Lexi flung her arms around Amanda and squeezed her tight.

"Thank you, thank you, thank you," Amanda whispered in her ear. Then, before she broke down completely, she hurried to the car. As they drove away, Amanda waved until the car disappeared from sight.

Mrs. Leighton was standing on the top step dabbing at her eyes. "Oh, my, this is harder than I expected it would be. I thought I could manage to say goodbye but . . ."

"You've still got me!" Lexi protested.

"Me, too!" Ben yelped, hanging on to his mother's leg.

"And us!" Jennifer, Binky and Egg chimed in.

Mrs. Leighton looked fondly at the five of them. "Then what am I doing out here?" she wondered. "I should be inside making you kids some snacks." She looked at Egg with an appraising eye. "I've got cookies made, and a cake, but you look thin, Egg. Would you like a sandwich? Cold meatloaf on bread?" she put her arm around the boy and drew him into the house. "Have you been eating well? You aren't working too hard in school, are you?"

"She's at it again," Lexi groaned. "Mothering."

"It's in her blood," Binky concluded. "I guess you're just stuck with one great mother."

Lexi smiled and nodded as she led her friends into the house.

———

Book Number Seven in the Cedar River Daydreams Series:

It's a time of "firsts" for Binky. Her first boyfriend, her first job as a part-time nanny, and her first truly serious decision to be made. She suspects someone in the family for whom she babysits of child abuse. What should she do? What can she do?

A Note From Judy

I'm glad you're reading *Cedar River Daydreams*! I hope I've given you something to think about as well as a story to entertain you. If you feel you have any of the problems that Lexi and her friends experience, I encourage you to talk with your parents, a pastor, or a trusted adult friend. There are many people who care about you!

Also, I enjoy hearing from my readers, so if you'd like to write, my address is:

Judy Baer
Bethany House Publishers
6820 Auto Club Road
Minneapolis, MN 55438

Please include an addressed, stamped envelope if you would like an answer. Thanks.